Faerie Hearts

A Romantic Fantasy Collection

USA Today Bestselling Author
Anthea Sharp

Faerie Hearts collection copyright 2023 by Anthea Sharp. All rights reserved. Characters are fictional figments of the author's imagination. Please do not copy, upload, or distribute in any fashion.

Want to make sure you hear about Anthea's new books? Join her newsletter, and get a *free* short story when you sign up! Find out more at www.antheasharp.com

Cover by Ravven

Copyediting by Editing720 and Violagin

Ebook ISBN: 9781680131598

Paperback ISBN: 9781681581

QUALITY CONTROL: We care about producing error-free books. If you discover a typo or formatting issue, please contact antheasharp@hotmail so that it may be corrected.

CONTENTS

About the Stories	xi
THE FAERIE MAIDEN OF THE OAKS	1
HEART OF THE FOREST	65
The Gift of Love	119
THE SALT PRINCESS	143
THE WITCH OF THE WOODS	183
Acknowledgments	269
Also by Anthea Sharp	271
About the Author	273

Thank You, Kickstarter Backers!

~ Top Supporters ~

Mari C. Bell
Cynthia M Coffman
Devon

~ Romantics ~

Alisa Chan
Amethyst Dragonfly
Beth Caudill
Bree
Caitlin Millsaps
Caroline Atkins
Catherine (Cat) Maenzo
Donald
drgnldy71
Felicia MacLaren
Holly Colvin
Jennifer Grzankowski
Jeremy Reppy
Jill Bridgeman
Julianne
Kamber McKnight
Katie Heinlein
Kerry
Kristina A. S.
Lauren Freeman
Leslie B.
Liz the Great
Logan U.
Mark Posey
Mary Jo Rabe
Michelle L
Midnightmare
Rob Minney
Rose Fournier
Vicky S.
Wendy Alvarez
Xiomara Reyes

~ Fae Elves ~

Alex Maziarz
Danae
Emma Radovich
Jackie Kilby
Jasmine N
Kara Stogsdill
KittenMarie
Leah N. Atkinson
Melissa Williams
Monica Leonelle
Nicole Akeroyd-Slater
Ragnar McFarland
Shiann Gilley
Thordis Jensen
Tjalara Draper

~ Mer-Fae ~

@Jeffrey.Tristan.Thyme
A Family of Appalachian Faeries
Adrienne Romani
Aletia
Amanda Ecker
Anonymous

Anonymous Reader
Ashleigh Floyd
Astridd
Brenda Hiatt
Cara M
Cathy Peper
Chris Munroe
Christina H.
Christina Phillips
Clarissa
Courtney Delgado
Crystal Palumbo
Cynthia Waldron
Dead Fishie
Deborah Cooke
Easter Christopher
Eileen Mueller
Eric Brann
Eric W Swett
Erin Ratelle
Eva Holmquist
Haleigh Kirch
Hana Correa
Hannah Dodson
Jesikah Sundin
Kanyon K.
Karen Bulgarelli
KB Anne
Kellen Harkins
Kellie N.
Kitty M
Kristen Bellio
Laura Dahmer-White
Laura Sofia
Leilani Love
Lisa Silverthorne
Liz

Meghan Edwards
Meyari McFarland
Mikaeli
nashan
Natasha Raine McGrath
NeonPixxius
Nikole C.
Phoenix Grey
Pjk
Polina "polinchka" Bazlova
PunkARTchick
Ruthenia
Raven Storm
Reka
Rochelle Kurth
S.N. Keirstead
Sara Ontiveros
Sarah
Scott Casey
Steff Inada
TC Ross
Tish Thawer
Tracy Langcake
Vera Soroka
Vickie Grider
Wizard Flight

~ Print Fae ~

Aimee
Alexa Ward
Alice Hanov
Amanda Curley
Amey Zeigler
Annie Reed
Billye Herndon

Courtney
Dean Wesley Smith
ElBin
Heather
Katherine Shipman
KC McCormick Çiftçi
Lilith Darville
Louise Bergin
Maricela Ramirez
Mary Kennedy
Merrie Destefano
Ms. Georg Rice
Nicole Perkins
Nicolette Andrews
Nikki Jefford
Randy Mick
Rebecca Garcia
Richard Valdez
Scott Chisholm
Serena M
Stephany Ezard
T.L. Branson
Vancil Thomas

~ Digital Fae ~

Anonymous
Author Candace Osmond
Catherine Holmes
Céline Malgen
Claudia Klein
Dayle Dermatis
Debbie Mumford
Didi Kanjahn
Dobi Cross
E. R. Paskey
E.V. Everest
Eron Wyngarde
Jay Ishino
Jo Holloway
Johanna Rothman
John Shrek Walters
Jordan S.
Joyce Engel
Judith Everett
Jules C
Kat James
Katy Manck – BooksYALove
Leslie Claire Walker
Leslie Twitchell
Linda Niehoff
Lotus Goldstein
Lu
Lyn Perry
Mandy Wetherhold
Marie Andreas
Marie Devey
Meghan DiMarco
Natalie
Olivia Hardin
R.S. Kellogg
R.W. Wallace
Rachel P.
Raphael Bressel
Riki
Robert L. Slater
S Ross Hamilton
S.R. Jaye
Seána Green
Sharina Brock
Tenna C.
Teralyn Mitchell
Thorn Coyle
Victoria Price

For all you romantics at heart ~

ABOUT THE STORIES

The Faerie Maiden of the Oaks
Based on an Irish legend, a fey woman marries the human lord who has captured her heart. But beware faerie bargains…

Heart of the Forest
A prince becomes lost in a mystical forest, where he must fight for his life at the side of a moon-haired elf maiden who may hold the answer to his dreams.

The Gift of Love
Whether it's romantic love, or the deep ties of family, a perceptive young woman works to heal the hurts of a wounded heart.

Princess of Salt
When a princess tells her father the truth, he banishes her from his castle. She must face many trials to regain the acceptance of her family, and win back her true love.

The Witch of the Woods
Appearances can be deceiving, in this fairytale retelling of an old favorite with an unexpected twist.

THE FAERIE MAIDEN OF THE OAKS

INTRODUCTION

Maire Rua of Leamanagh Castle in County Clare, Ireland, is a fearsome figure of legend from the mid-1600s. According to the tales, she was bloodthirsty and scheming—a powerful red-haired woman who accompanied her husband, Conor, on raids against the English and who bore him eight children. After his death, she was reputed to have married and killed dozens of husbands (though historians agree that such accounts are untrue). The legends say she met her end by being imprisoned by her enraged enemies in the trunk of a hollow tree.

But why? Such myths don't spring up out of nothing.

Who, or *what*, was Maire Rua? What could have driven her to such acts, and were they really as terrible as the legends say, or is there a different explanation—a different tale to be told?

After combing through a dozen different stories regarding Maire Rua; including ones that claimed she married twenty-five husbands but divorced them all after a year and a day, that she threw one husband out the castle window and tricked another into riding a blind horse over the cliffs and into the sea, and that she frequently rode with her husband Conor O'Brien (descended from legendary kings) into battle, I believe another truth has emerged.

That tale is below. It is up to you to decide where history and legend intersect. And if you ever visit the ruins of Leamanagh Castle, on the edge of the limestone plain of the Burren, listen closely.

You might hear the laughter of a faerie woman and a once-mortal man in the sigh of the wind whistling about their abandoned manor house. You might glimpse a shimmer of red hair disappearing through a shadowed doorway hidden within an oak tree.

But if you do see such a thing, it would be better not to follow...

CHAPTER 1

IN THE REALM OF FAERIE where the Bright Court gives way to the Dusklands, a fae woman waited. She was tall, as all spirits of the trees are, her red hair the color of a mortal sunset. The grove of trees encircling her rustled quietly in the wind, and overhead a few stars shone, never waxing or waning. Only the crescent moon sailed that gray charcoal sky, on its way to preside over the fey and midnight creatures of the Dark Court.

The woman stood, as still as the oak at her back. Finally, after a heartbeat or an eternity, the distant sound of a hunting horn rippled through the air. She swayed and closed her eyes, as green as new leaves in springtime. Then she turned and laid her hand upon the crinkled bark of the oak tree.

A door appeared, a soundless opening into darkness. With a feral smile, she stepped though.

"The faerie woman of the wood, is it?" The tavern keeper shook his head and plunked two flagons of ale onto the scarred wooden table. "Best take care, Conor O'Brien."

Conor glanced up at the man. "I never asked for your opinion, Fergal. Let alone overhearing a private conversation."

"Aye, well." Fergal wiped his hands on the grubby apron tied about his waist. "If you bring trouble to Munster, we know who to blame."

"The English are already here," Conor's companion, Teige, said darkly, grabbing his ale and taking a long draught.

"There's trouble, and then there's *trouble*," the tavern keeper said.

"Leave me to choose my own, then." Conor cocked an eyebrow at the man, then turned back to his friend, pointedly ignoring Fergal.

With a loud sigh, the tavern keeper went to tend his other patrons. No doubt he'd serve up the gossip alongside the red ale he brewed in the cellar. But there was little harm done. Few men would seek out the fair folk of their own accord.

Then again, Conor had always been outside the ordinary. It came, his mother had said, from being descended from Brain Boru, the greatest chieftain Ireland had ever known.

"I'm going to the grove tomorrow," Conor said. "Perhaps I'll catch sight of her again."

It was nearly Samhain Eve, the night when the old year turned to the new and the doors between the worlds opened,

Teige gave him a mournful look. "And when you don't return? When the fair folk snatch you away into their realm, what then? Who will become lord of Leamanagh Castle?"

"I'll return," Conor said, with more confidence than he should.

Still, he had no choice. His heart had been stolen, and he feared he would never get it back. But he must try.

CHAPTER 2

Conor had glimpsed the red-haired woman a fortnight earlier, and since then all his dreams had been filled with her. It made sense to him now why no maiden of village or keep had been able to catch his fancy. He'd been waiting. For *her*.

The day had been cold. For most of the October afternoon, rain had sleeted down across the countryside, slicking the rocks of the Burren and turning the bogs even more sodden. He and his men had been returning from an unsuccessful hunt when a mist had sprung up, thickening the air until they could scarcely see one another.

Between one breath and the next, his men were gone, as truly as if they'd been spirited away into another world. Conor was alone. Despite calling his companions' names into the white air, no reply came. He took the hunting horn from beneath his cloak and blew it. The echoes came back eerily, as if mocking him.

But Conor O'Brien was not a man to let such things throw him into despair. He kept to the direction they'd been heading, back toward the castle. When his horse stumbled, he dismounted to spare the animal a fall over the difficult ground, and led the creature along.

Dusk came early, and as the light faded, Conor couldn't help the first prickles of fear between his shoulder blades.

Men could get lost in the dark, wander into a fen or over a cliff, never to be seen again. Perhaps he should halt, make a rude camp upon the stony plain, and wait for morning.

He was casting about for a suitable spot when he heard music just at the edge of his senses—a fey harping coming from a short distance away. Though part of him knew there was no crofter's cottage in the area, the promise of a warm fire and refuge from the night pulled him on.

He rounded an outcropping of rock to discover he'd come to one of the scattered oak groves that edged the plain. Light shone from the center of the trees, turning the bare silhouettes to fantastical, frightening shapes. It was not the warm orange flicker Conor had been hoping for, but a cool radiance that was neither blue nor golden but somewhere in between.

Still, it was better than nothing.

He approached carefully, trying to make as little noise as possible. Halting at the edge of the oaks, he tethered his horse to a low branch, then crept forward to see where the strange light was coming from. The sound of music was louder now, ethereal and wild.

It was nothing from the mortal world, that was certain. And though he knew meddling with the fair folk was perilous, his curiosity drew him onward.

I'll just see what's there, he told himself. Surely a quick look would do no harm before he made a wise retreat. If he glimpsed a faerie, it would make a fine tale to boast of around the fire.

A small clearing lay at the center of the grove. Pulse beating in his throat, Conor fetched up behind the nearest oak, then slowly peered around the side. The breath stilled in his throat and his fingers tightened on the rough bark when he saw the maiden seated in the clearing.

She was perched on a hewn stone, a harp in her lap. Her pale, graceful fingers danced over the strings, plucking out a melody. The golden-blue radiance filled the air, coming from nowhere and everywhere, and in that light the long fall of her red hair looked like a sheet of frozen fire.

Despite his caution, he must have made some sound or movement, for she abruptly stopped playing. The silence echoing in his ears, she lifted her head and looked straight at him. Her eyes were an impossible color: greener than the fields of Ireland, greener than the clearest of emeralds.

His heart clenched, filled with such hope and yearning as he'd never felt before.

"Who is spying on me?" she asked, her voice amused yet cool. "Come out from the trees mortal, so I might look at you."

Taking his courage in his two hands, he stepped out from the shelter of the woods. But though he might have shown himself, Conor knew better than to give any of the fair folk his true name.

"You can call me MacDonogh," he said. "Who are you?"

She laughed. "Do you think I'm so easily entrapped as that, mortal man? Why should I tell you such a thing?"

He took another step forward, his gaze never leaving her

face. "So that, as I lie upon my deathbed after a lifetime of pining for a red-haired faerie maiden, I'll know what name to carry with me into the West."

Her laugh was a silvery thing, like a flight of swallows dipping and turning in the air.

"Such flattery! And how do you think you'll be welcomed into Tir na nÓg?"

"As a warrior." He lifted his chin, one hand going to the sword at his side.

Already his men had carried out a successful number of raids against the marauding English, and he'd sworn not to rest until they were driven back to their own country.

"The mortal world is filled with warriors."

"As a poet, then."

She shook her head. "You are not yet mad enough to be a poet."

"If I look upon you long enough, I will be." The words lay true in his mouth. Already he could feel a bit of his soul torn off, forever lost to the green-eyed faerie maid.

She tipped her head, the light sliding off the red blaze of her hair. "Perhaps. Though a bard might do better."

"I've little skill upon the harp. But for you, lady, I will pledge my days to practice until my fingers bleed and my voice is harsh as a raven's."

"Nay." She set her harp aside and stood. "Let me read your face, MacDonogh, to see what future is written therein."

He stood, transfixed, as she moved toward him, as graceful as the wind over a field of barley. As she approached she carried with her the piquant scent of acorns and rain-drenched moss.

Beware! his senses sang. To gaze into a faerie woman's eyes was to court madness, indeed.

But then he would be a poet, and would devote his life to finding her again.

She halted a hands' breadth from him, so close that a strand of her hair blew between them and tickled his cheek. It was all he could do to hold himself still, quivering like a stag within the hunter's sights.

It was not a feeling he was much accustomed to—yet he bore it, for her sake. Any sudden move would drive her away, no matter how much he yearned to lean forward and touch the white velvet of her skin, the silken flame of her hair.

"Ah." She leaned forward, the warmth of her breath nearly pushing him to his knees with yearning. "You have a destiny laid before you, son of chieftains."

She held his gaze, looking deeply into his eyes a long moment. Then, suddenly, she flinched away, as though she'd seen something terrible.

"What is it?" he asked, reaching after her as she ran lightly back to the center of the clearing.

She scooped up her harp, then pointed. "Your home lies in that direction, mortal man. Never come this way again."

"Wait," he cried, even as the light grew so bright he had to shield his eyes.

He stumbled forward, knocking his shins upon the stone where she'd sat. But she was gone. A moment later, the eerie glow faded until he stood alone in a dark grove.

Had she been a dream?

He turned slowly, scanning the trees, but there was no sign that a faerie woman had ever graced the clearing. The darkness rustled with shadows, the bare limbs of the oaks creaking together as if mocking him.

Sorrow aching in his chest, Conor trudged back to his horse. It took half the night to find his way home to Leamanagh. But later, taking the brooch from his cloak, he discovered a single strand of long red hair tangled in the pin. Hair the color of sunset.

The color of a heart forever wounded.

"What have you done, tree-maiden?" the banshee hissed, the hollow sockets of her eyes filled with shadows. "Even *I* felt the ripples over the Realm from your foolish visit to the mortal world."

The faerie maiden leaned against the oak, pulling strength from the rough bark. When she'd stepped back through the doorway, the banshee known as Aibell had been waiting.

"I felt a calling to step across the worlds," the maiden said.

It was true. A restless desire had run through her, like sap quickening in the springtime; a compulsion to slip through the door in the oak and into the human realm.

Where she'd met a man with hair the color of night and eyes the blue of a stormy lake, who had not flinched from her, nor attempted to clutch her to him, though she could feel the desire running just beneath his skin.

He was brave, too, and well-spoken. Not many mortals would have borne themselves with such honor.

And then she'd read something in his eyes—a shadow of death, a twining of their fates that had frightened her more than words could tell.

"You threaten the balance," the banshee said. "Even now the emissaries of the Dark Court and the Bright are coming. Do you not hear them?"

The maiden lifted her head, then shivered as she heard the hounds of the Wild Hunt circle overhead, baying. Through the trees, the chime of silver bells announced the arrival of the Bright King's knight.

She turned, poised to flee. For a reckless moment she considered taking refuge in the human world. But that way lay her own destruction. A faerie of the oakwood could never survive alone among mortals, especially with both courts of the Realm in pursuit. When the Wild Hunt found her, as they inevitably would, they would tear her to pieces.

Reluctantly, she turned back to face the dark figure of the Huntsman and the knight in golden armor. Perhaps, between the two of them, they would show her some mercy.

"I am here to bid you attend my Queen," the Huntsman said in a deep voice.

"And I am here to bring you to my King," the knight countered. "For you have broken the laws of the Realm, and must answer."

"I broke no laws," the maiden said, her heartbeat fluttering, though her words were steady. "I only paid a brief visit to the human world."

"And left something behind," the Huntsman said. "For that, you must pay the price."

"I left nothing!"

"Ah, but you did." The golden knight shook his head. "Even now, the man who called himself MacDonogh carries a strand of your hair next to his heart."

Her hand went to her long hair. "But... I never meant to."

The banshee laughed, a high screeching sound. "You're as foolish as the humans who stumble into our snares, *an darach*. Fate doesn't care what you mean to do."

"What brings you here, Aibell?" The Huntsman turned his antlered helm toward the banshee. "This is no business of yours."

"Ah, but it concerns the death of an O'Brien," she said. "And so it is my business, after all."

The oak maiden caught her breath—though she had seen it in his eyes, that bold, brave mortal's life snuffed out like a candle in a gust of wind.

"He's going to die?"

Another cackle from the banshee. "They all do. The question is simply *when*. Your actions have hastened his end."

The thought of his death was like an arrow of sorrow, sharp-tipped through her chest. She knew it was perilous for humans to encounter her kind, but she'd never thought her mere presence might spell doom. Especially to a man as fair and well-spoken as the one she'd met in the oak wood.

"How might I reverse the harm I've done?" she asked softly.

Though she'd spent only a handful of moments with the man calling himself MacDonagh, she felt as though she knew him from some long-ago time. She'd read their entwined destinies in the depths of his eyes. He couldn't die—not yet! Not when all they knew of one another was a shared smile beneath the oaks.

"Ah." The golden knight nodded, starlight shimmering off his armor. "'Twould be fitting to weave your amends and punishment together. Would you not agree, Huntsman?"

"That depends on the punishment," the antlered hunter said. "It must not be too easy."

"Banish her back to the mortal world," Aibell said. "She can safeguard the man until the hour of his true death."

"Then what?" the Huntsman asked.

"Then"—the banshee's smile stretched evilly across her gaunt face—"she must remain among the humans until she has wed five-and-twenty men and sent each one to their doom."

The Huntsman laughed, low and hollow, but the Bright King's emissary shook his head. "That is too heavy a burden. She must remain married to each man for a year and a day, after which they will be free to go about their lives."

"And if they leave me before that time?" the maiden asked in a quiet voice.

She tried to smother the despair washing through her at the thought of her long banishment. At the thought of so many deaths—starting with the man whom she'd inadvertently doomed. The man who had stirred such feelings in her that she'd been forced to flee, carelessly leaving a strand of her hair behind.

"Then your faithless husbands will pay the price," the Huntsman said.

"So you'd best be a trusty wife." The banshee turned to stare at her. "I can tell you now, you will not always succeed."

"I will do my best." The maiden lifted her chin. "And after those five-and-twenty marriages, I demand to return to the Realm, and be reunited with my first love."

"You ask that the mortal be taken here upon his death?" The knight frowned beneath the golden filigree of his helm.

"I do." She stared defiantly back at him. "Otherwise, I will not accept your punishment, but instead go and throw myself into the sea."

The banshee let out a laugh. "Never underestimate the stubbornness of an oak tree."

"But is the mortal even worthy of such an honor?" the knight persisted.

"He is," Aibell said, unexpectedly changing allegiances. "He is descended from kings, and is destined to die in battle. It would not be the first time such a warrior came to dwell in the Realm of Faerie upon departing the mortal world."

"In that case, on behalf of the Bright Court, I agree," the knight said.

The antlered Hunstman looked at Aibell. "Not all her husbands will escape unscathed?"

"Nay." The banshee had no need to say more. As a harbinger of death, she could read the fates of mortals more clearly than any of the fey folk.

"Then, as emissary of the Dark Court, I, too will accept those terms." The Huntsman turned to the faerie maid. "Will you be bound, oak-maiden?"

Slowly, the faerie nodded. After her true love's death, twenty-five years in the mortal world would pass quickly in the Realm. She had no fear her husband would forget her while she toiled to satisfy the terms of her punishment, though it might feel like an eternity to her.

"I accept," she said.

The toll of a deep bell shivered over the landscape, and the envoys of the Dark Court and the Bright nodded.

"It is done," the golden knight said. "A true binding."

"My Queen will be satisfied." The Huntsman bowed his head, his tall antlers dipping against the star-dusted sky.

"Now go, tree-maiden," the knight commanded. "We shall seal the doorway behind you. It will not open again until your geas is fulfilled."

She pulled in a last, deep breath of the enchanted air of the Realm. Then she turned, set her hand upon the oak, and walked through the doorway to meet her fate.

CHAPTER 3

SAMHAIN EVE LAID long shadows over the land as Conor rode across the plain toward the oak grove. It was an auspicious time for doorways to open, and he planned to arrive at dusk, to improve his chances of glimpsing the red-haired maiden.

You know nothing of her, his common sense insisted. *Perhaps she's only luring you to your doom—a blood sacrifice to stain her hair a deeper red.*

The thought sent a momentary shiver down his spine.

But no. If the faerie woman wished him ill, she'd had plenty of chances to harm him upon their first meeting. Instead, she'd gazed deeply into his eyes, and then shown him the direction home.

Still, what would he do if she was there? What if she wasn't?

Well, then. He gave himself a shake. Even when dealing with magical folk, one could think sensibly.

If she appeared in the grove, as he hoped, he would ask her to stay. To marry him, as a life without her seemed a relentlessly dreary prospect. It wouldn't be the first time a mortal man had come home with a fey bride, though the men of the sea were more often returning with selkie-maids than warriors with maidens from the oak grove.

A faerie of the trees was a different thing, surely—but if she consented, he would be a happy man. And if she did not, he would spend the rest of his days an unhappy one, plagued with bitter yearning.

Indeed, if she didn't appear, he was of half a mind to try and make his own way into the Realm of Faerie in search of her. Despite what Teige had said, there were other heirs to Leamanagh Castle. None as well-suited as Conor, true, but the place wouldn't fall to ruin. Not for centuries yet, if ever.

Who wouldn't want to dwell in the Realm of Faerie? Even if it turned a man mad, Conor thought that fate might not be so terrible. There was only thin line between madness and ecstasy, after all. What might look like lunacy from one side could well be transportations of bliss on the other.

He was willing to take that chance, provided a doorway opened.

Much to his relief, as he approached the oak grove he glimpsed the blue-gold light flickering above the trees. The sound of a harp drifted through the air, beckoning him on, and the wind rustled the bare branches of the oaks. This time, they didn't seem to be mocking him, but whispering encouragement.

Conor dismounted and led his horse beneath the trees, his boots crunching over the curls of brown leaves. If the faerie maid agreed to go with him, he would put her up on the back of his mount and they would ride home together.

She must have heard his approach, for the harping ceased.

When he stepped into the clearing, she stood there, waiting. His horse made a soft snort, but didn't seem minded to flee.

"Greetings, fair maiden." Conor made her a bow. "I had hoped to see you this night."

She tilted her head, her green eyes sweeping over him from head to toe. "I might say the same, mortal man."

"And why would that be?" he asked, his throat tightening with hope. With fear.

If she meant to harm him, this would be the time. His gaze flicked to her hands, which lay empty at her sides, no sharp thorn or other weapon concealed within the curve of her long, graceful fingers. Not that a faerie woman needed aught but magic to bring him down.

Uncertainty moved across her expression, making her suddenly seem almost mortal. Conor took a step forward. The silence settled, and in its depths he thought he heard a single bell toll.

"I am here," the woman said at last, "to keep your doom from you, O'Brien."

He pulled in a startled breath, the air hissing through his teeth. "How do you know my name?"

"It is known in the Realm," she said, which was no answer at all.

"Then I must thank you for your care, for any man would wish to have his fate averted. Yet I must ask. Why?"

She glanced away, her red hair falling down to cover her cheek. When she raised her head to meet his gaze again, there was a spark of sorrow in her eyes.

"Because, by seeing me here in the wood the other day, I hastened the hour of your death."

He shivered at the words. Was he to fall down the next instant, stone cold upon the ground?

"How long do I have, then?" The question rasped his throat.

A half-smile lifted one corner of her wide mouth, and she took a step forward. "Fear not, mortal man. You are in no imminent danger. But beyond that, I cannot say, though I believe there are years yet left to you."

Years. He supposed it was better than months. The cold breath of his fate braced his courage. For if every man died, why not reach for happiness with both hands while he still lived?

"I see." He lifted his chin. "My name is Conor O'Brien. And whatever days I might have left, I'd spend them with you."

The wind stilled, as if the trees of the grove held their breaths.

"That is why I am here," she said softly.

A bright jab of hope went through him, a falling star diving from the impossible heavens toward the earth.

"Might I have a name to call you with, faerie maid?"

She hesitated a moment. "In my land, I am called *Mirawen'-tavaril*."

It was a lovely, liquid name, and nothing mortal about it whatsoever. Conor shook his head, thinking a moment as he turned the syllables over on his tongue.

"Might I call you Maire?" he asked. "It's a human name, but close enough to the start of your own that you might find it acceptable."

"Mai..." She trailed off, watching him closely.

"Maire."

"Maire," she repeated. "Yes. It will do. But what of a following name? Is that not the mortal custom?"

"It is, but"—he held out his hand—"most often the wife takes her husband's name. Will you take mine, Maire-of-the-wood?"

She smiled, and it was the dawn breaking over the fields. Gently, she set her hand in his. All the questions clamoring inside him settled.

He knew not how long they might have together, but he would savor every moment.

CHAPTER 4

THE FAERIE MAIDEN, newly named Maire, clutched her husband-to-be's shoulders as they rode into Castle Leamanagh. Full night had fallen as they headed over the rocky plain, and now torchlight flickered, orange and red, at the wooden gate of her new home.

She wasn't certain what she'd expected from a mortal castle. Not the glowing halls of the Bright Court, nor the tangled briars of the Dark, to be sure. But as she stared up at the square stone tower rising over the muddy courtyard, her spirits plummeted. In the back of her mind she heard the banshee's cackle.

What life had she chosen for herself?

Yet there was no choice but to go forward. She glanced at the firelit edge of Conor O'Brien's jaw, the dark hair falling over his cheek, and took a deep breath. She knew not why her heartbeat raced when she gazed upon him. They were strangers to one another, she of the fair folk and he a mortal man. Their worlds could not be more different.

And yet they fit together, like dark and light, like waking and sleeping—each one necessary for the other to exist.

"What do you think of my castle?" Conor asked as he pulled the horse to a halt. "I know it's likely not what you're used to, but I hope to make you happy here."

"I will be happy," she answered, though she feared the road would be difficult. Yet what more could she say?

He glanced back at her, questions in his stormy blue eyes, but a moment later they were surrounded by his people. A handful of fighters dressed in leathers with swords at their sides, a woman wearing a flour-dusted apron, another still holding her spindle, and a small flock of children who stared at her hair, their eyes wide in the flickering torchlight. *Rua*, they whispered. Red.

"Ah, you've done it now," a tall warrior said, glancing at Maire and shaking his head.

"I told you all would be well, Teige." Conor grinned, then held up his hand to still the babble of questions. "This is Maire. We're to be wed on the morrow, at the dawning of the new year."

His words were met with shocked silence, but his smile didn't falter as he slid from his mount. Turning, he helped her down. His hands were warm on her waist, and she leaned close to him, trying not to let the strangeness overwhelm her. Already she could feel the mud seeping through the birchbark soles of her slippers.

"What are you thinking, Conor O'Brien, to be bringing such as *she* within these walls?" An old woman stepped forward, leaning on a stout stick. "If you've misjudged, none of us will see the sunrise."

Stung, Maire stared back at her. "I'm no unseelie woman, planning to murder you all in your beds."

The old woman bent forward, her hands clasped on her stick, her eyes narrowed. "Then what *are* you?"

"The woman who saved my life." Conor stepped between them. "I'll not hear a word against my bride. If you don't like it, Doireen, there are other holdings you can go serve."

"You'd turn me out onto the Burren, at my age?" Doireen scowled at him. "After my parents served your grandfather, and generations more, besides? Nay, I'll stay. But make no mistake"—she turned her glare on Maire—"my eye will be upon you, lass."

"Gran." A younger, brown-haired woman stepped forward. "Is this how we treat guests to the castle? You all ought to be ashamed. I bid you welcome, milady."

She curtsied to Maire—a rough human bow, nothing like the elegant court curtsies of the fae, but all the more friendly for it.

Maire nodded back, unsure of whether to return the bow.

"Thank you, Cara," Conor said. "See to a room for my new bride, if you will. And we'll take a bite of supper in the hall."

Cara beckoned to the other women clustered about, and they headed back into the towering keep. With a last, baleful glance, Doireen stumped after them.

"My lady?" Conor held his arm out to Maire.

Gratefully, she slipped her hand around his elbow and let him lead her to the arched door. Just before they passed through, she glanced up the wall of stone. It was marked by strange narrow openings that served some purpose she couldn't guess. There was only one window, perched near the very top of the tower.

Inside the cavernous hall, the air was dim and smoky. Oil lanterns were arrayed on long tables, more torches flickered on the walls, and a great hearth at the center of the room cast warmth and ruddy light. A passage beside the hearth led back to what Maire guessed were the food preparation areas.

She would need to eat of mortal food, herself. No more taking nourishment from the earth and sky—not when she was banished to the mortal world, trapped in a mortal form.

A faerie such as herself could slip from maiden to tree between one heartbeat and the next. But not here. Even if the terms of her punishment permitted it—which they did not— to perform such magic would only make the humans fear and distrust her.

More than they already did, that was.

At least Conor seemed content to seat her at his side on one of the long benches fronting the tables. The warrior, Teige, settled across from them. His dark gaze fell heavily on Maire, judging her.

She straightened her shoulders and returned his weighted gaze with one of her own.

Conor looked between them, and let out a laugh. "Warriors, the both of you. Beware, Teige, or she'll take your place beside me in battle."

The words were said in jest, but she turned to her bridegroom. "I will ride with you whenever you go to war. Though it's not my intention to displace any of your loyal men."

Conor's smile faded as he looked at her for a long moment. "You mean it."

"I do." She stared deeply into his eyes, so that he would understand the truth of it. "I didn't give up my own world simply to come here and watch you ride off to your doom."

"Hm." Teige's brows rose. "A fierce lass at your side is no bad thing. Perhaps I should go out to the oak grove myself, and see what I might bring home."

"A gnarled old hag, if you're lucky," Conor said, but Maire shook her head.

"It will only hasten your ruin," she said. "Even if you meet another faerie within those trees—which is most unlikely—they wouldn't be of any help to you. I'm only able to save Conor because he's descended from kings."

"Sometimes I might hate you a little, O'Brien," Teige said, but there was not a hint of dislike in his voice.

Maire frowned slightly. How long would it take before humans made sense to her?

Well, she supposed she had years ahead of her to find out.

CHAPTER 5

AFTER A SMALL BUT flavorful supper of bread and stew, Cara came to the hall to show Maire to her room. Conor rose and pressed Maire's hand. His fingers were warm over hers, and the worry that had been building within her eased at his touch.

"Sleep well," he said gently, as though he sensed her trepidation. "If you need anything at all, ask."

She nodded mutely. Until she'd spent more time in the human world, she had no idea what she might require. Of a certainty, the castle could not provide her with spun cobwebs to wear upon her body, or honey-sap for nourishment.

A harp, perhaps. She'd set hers down upon the stone before agreeing to go with Conor, and when she'd turned back, it was gone. Like faerie gold, precious things from the Realm vanished under the light of the mortal sun.

But now was not the time to be making demands. The people of Castle Leamanagh already distrusted her, and imperious orders would only harden their hearts against her. Besides, Maire was no court fae, accustomed to lesser folk doing her bidding. She was used to tending to herself—though what that meant in the mortal world, she couldn't be sure.

Cara led her out of the firelit warmth of the lower hall to a stone staircase set against the far wall. A few wrought metal sconces burned at intervals, and by their spotty light and the lantern Cara held, they ascended. They spiraled up three flights, and at each landing they passed a niche ending in one of the slitted openings in the outer walls. Despite their oilcloth coverings, cool air seeped into the castle

"What are those for?" Maire finally asked.

Cara gave her a curious look. "For archers. Have you no fortified castles in… your country?"

"Not like this, no."

Judging from Cara's question, Maire guessed that no one would openly come out and say that Conor's new bride was from the Realm of Faerie. They'd simply pretend she was from some foreign land, which was true enough.

Finally, they reached the upper floor of the tower, where a long hall stretched down to a glass-paned window. The lantern light showed their reflections—herself pale and tall, her hair like a flame, and Cara, short and brown-haired, a serious look on her face.

They walked over a yellow and green carpet. On their left stretched the outer stone wall, but the right boasted paneled dark wood set with carved doors.

"This is to be your room," Cara said, halting midway down the corridor. "His lordship's is just beyond."

She opened the door, then stood back so that Maire could enter.

Her new home. Cautiously, she stepped inside, unsure of what to expect.

The walls were made of polished wood, with a tapestry hanging on one side depicting a flowery forest where laughing people rode between the trees. A lantern was set on a table near the bed, and the bed itself bore green brocade curtains, like swags of ornate moss draped from the posts.

Indeed, in some ways it put her in mind of her own tree-heart dwelling, and she felt her worries ease once again.

"It's lovely," she told Cara, who was hovering anxiously at her shoulder.

A peat fire burned on the small hearth, and though Maire was not overfond of flames, she knew she must become accustomed to them. Mortals could not conjure light, or move with ease through the starlit dark, so fire must be their ally. Even if it was not hers.

A peat fire, however, smoldered and didn't leap hungrily upon wood, and neither did the lantern light, which fed steadily upon oil. So, it would be tolerable to live with the constant presence of fire. And she had to admit she was glad of the warmth it provided, as it was clear she'd come to the human world during the colder part of the year.

"Do you need help preparing for bed?" Cara asked.

Maire cocked her head. "What kind of aid might I require?"

"Undoing the lacings of your gown, brushing out your hair and braiding it for sleep, donning your nightdress." Cara gestured to a handful of garments hanging in a tall cupboard. "We found you a few things to wear, as you can see. Banking the fire, turning out the lantern, closing the bed curtains—"

"Then yes," Maire said. "This is all much more complicated

than I'm used to. I would welcome your assistance."

"Good." Cara returned her smile and set the lantern down beside the door. "Doireen said you're too full of cunning and strangeness and that I shouldn't offer, but she was wrong."

"I am not cunning, but I do feel strange," Maire admitted as she looked about her room once more.

"Well and who wouldn't? Now sit, and I'll do your hair." Cara gestured to a cushioned bench set before a low table.

Since it was expected of her, Maire took a seat and surveyed the items arrayed on the table. A silver-backed hairbrush and comb, a large mirror set in an oval frame, a length of green ribbon and a few handfuls of string. To tie back her hair, she supposed.

Cara took up the brush and began lightly running it through Maire's hair. It was not unpleasant, though no one but herself had ever brushed her hair before. Like everything else in the mortal world, it would take some getting used to.

"What will the wedding be like, on the morrow?" she asked, glancing at Cara's reflection in the mirror.

"It will be a handfasting. There's no need to send to Ennis for a priest—especially in this instance." Cara paused and sent her a look. "Do you know anything about the ceremony?"

Maire shook her head, the motion tugging at the brush. Cara set it aside and began twisting her hair into a braid.

"Well, don't worry. It's a simple enough thing, and then you'll be wed."

Maire would be wed—to Conor O'Brien, whose bold words and blue eyes had ensnared her, even to the point of leaving her own realm in order to save him. The thought of him made her heart beat faster, and in the mirror her reflection's cheeks went pink.

"I could ask for no better husband," she said softly.

"Aye—you'll be the envy of all of Munster," Cara said, grinning. "Now, off to bed with you, milady. Rest well, so that you might look your best on the morrow."

"Will you preside over the handfasting?" Conor asked Teige as the two of them sat drinking whiskey before the great hearth.

The hour was late, the castle quiet and the fire turning to coals. Conor had told his friend all the details of meeting Maire, and that their two fates were bound together, though he knew not why. The ways of the fair folk couldn't be argued with—and indeed, he had no mind to try.

"There's no turning back now, I suppose," Teige said, echoing Conor's thoughts.

"And why would I, when the most lovely maiden in all the world is about to become my bride?" Conor took a swallow of his whiskey, savoring the long burn of it down his throat.

"You won't reconsider? It seems a perilous thing, to wed a faerie maid."

"I'll embrace that peril—and the maiden, too. Besides, you saw how staunchly she promised to defend me."

Teige shook his head. "Will you really let her ride out with us to battle the English?"

"Do you think I could stop her?" Conor shot his friend a fierce smile. "No, our fates are bound together already. I just ask that you bind us as husband and wife."

"Then I'll do as you wish." Teige let out a sigh and turned to stare at the fire smoldering to coals in the hearth. "I only hope it doesn't bring ruin upon all our heads."

CHAPTER 6

MAIRE WOKE AT DAWN. For a moment, confusion raced through her and she twisted against the bedsheets, her heart pounding.

I am in the mortal world. The realization calmed her, though her pulse still throbbed in her throat. Faint light crept into the room around a heavy green curtain she hadn't noticed the night before. Rising, she went and pulled it aside to reveal a casement window recessed in the wall.

The sky was the cool gray of dawn, mirroring the limestone plain of the Burren stretching out from Leamanagh Castle.

Not a tree in sight. Maire smiled grimly, reaching with her senses for the nearest grove. It was some distance away, though not as far as her own sheltering oaks. Still, she would ask Conor if she might visit it now and then.

A tree-maiden could not thrive trapped forever on a rocky plain. Perhaps she might convince her new husband to plant some saplings. And add more windows to the keep, if such a thing were possible.

Foolish, she told herself. If she were asking for the impossible, she might as well request a whole new manor filled with light to be built adjoining the tower. And the moon and stars on top of that.

With a short laugh at her own folly, she turned from the window and went to look at the human clothing Cara had found for her. Two of the dresses were made of spun wool and dyed in subdued colors of dark blue and rusty red. The third was fashioned of a tapestry-like brocade in shades of old gold. Though each dress had a lace collar and puffed sleeves, they bore little resemblance to the gossamer green gown she'd arrived in.

She reached for the brocade gown. It was probably best if she didn't flaunt her fey origins, especially upon her wedding day.

～

As was the custom, Conor hadn't seen his bride-to-be that morning. He sought out Cara in the great hall to ask how Maire fared.

"Well enough," Cara said. "She had a good breakfast in her rooms. I'm about to go back up to help her prepare for the wedding."

"Bring her this, if you will." He reached into the pocket of his doublet—his most ornate one, embroidered with vines and *fleur de lis*—and pulled out a slender jewelry case.

Cara took it with a smile. "The family pendant, is it?"

He nodded. It was an elaborate piece of jewelry: a ruby droplet suspended from the jewel-encrusted figure of a mermaid, which in turn hung from three tiers of golden chains.

"It seems a fitting gift," he said.

As well as a reminder to the folk of Leamanagh Castle that Maire would be the new lady of the keep and he would stand beside her in all things.

"And what of a ring?" Cara gave him a close look.

"Of course I have a ring for her."

"I meant one that she might give *you*." There was an impatient note in her voice.

"Ah." He pursed his lips. "I admit, I hadn't given it any thought. But here."

He slipped off his heavy silver signet ring, engraved with the triple lions of the O'Brien crest, and handed it to Cara. In the usual course of things, the bride's family, or the groom's, would provide her with a ring for the ceremony. But Maire was alone in the world, and Conor's parents had passed some time ago. In the haste of the handfasting, such details had slipped his mind.

"I thank you for the reminder," he said to Cara as she turned to go. "Would you stand by my lady in the days to come?"

"Indeed, I shall," she said. "For all her strangeness, she's kind. I think she will do well as the Lady of Leamanagh."

Conor nodded, relieved to hear that Maire had another ally within the castle. Now to bring Doireen around—but given time, the old woman would see that no matter how fey, the new lady of the keep was nothing to fear.

To occupy his time until the ceremony, he retired to his study on the upper floor. As he passed by Maire's room, he heard her laugh, and his heart rose at the sound. He would do anything within his power to make her happy, his lovely faerie bride.

Even allowing her to ride out on the next raid against the English. There must be some leather armor they could modify for her. As for a weapon, he knew that the fair folk could not bear the touch of iron, but the armory still held some old bronze swords. He'd have his arms man put a sharp edge to one, and it should serve well enough.

Indeed, such a gift might make her even happier than the elaborate pendant, for surely she was accustomed to jewels and finery aplenty in her own land. But he wagered that very few of the fey folk bore a mortal blade.

"I'm sorry we've no flowers to weave into your hair," Cara said as she twined pearls about the braids pinned atop Maire's head. "Though I think one of the girls has a dried posy she can give you to carry."

"This will do very well," Maire said, though in truth she'd little notion of what a bride ought to look like.

Cara had approved of her choice of the gold brocade, and had helped her into the underdress and various other garments that humans wore beneath their clothing. It seemed rather a lot, though Maire supposed that in the cold winters such things were useful. The clammy air of Castle Leamanagh pressed against her.

The sound of a bell clanging drifted up to the window, and Cara hastily tucked the last of the pearl-strewn netting over Maire's head.

"Time for the handfasting," Cara said. "But first, his lordship sent you two things."

She held out a long, thin box fashioned of polished wood. Slowly, Maire opened it to see an opulent necklace nestled within on a bed of black velvet.

"This is lovely," she said, touching it with one finger.

It was jewelry fit for a queen, the gold chain gleaming softly. She lifted it up, smiling to see the figures of a moon and a mermaid fashioned of precious stones and gold. Despite being a tree-maiden, she would be happy to wear such a thing of beauty.

"I'll fasten it," Cara said, nodding at her to don the necklace.

Maire put the pendant on. It was heavy, but not an unpleasant burden. Much like her choice to come to the mortal world.

"What is the other thing you're to give me?" she asked.

"This." Cara held out a silver ring.

Maire took it, holding it up to the light. It was far too large to fit her own graceful fingers.

"For Conor?" she guessed.

"Aye." Cara smiled at her. "You'll make promises to one another, and exchange rings. Conor will tell you when. Now, we'd best go. A bride can't be *too* tardy to her wedding."

Now that the moment was nearly upon her, Maire's chest was filled with a flutter like fallen leaves scudding before the wind. Silently, she followed Cara down to the main hall. A blur of human faces watched her enter, and for a moment she felt dizzy.

Then Conor's storm-blue gaze met hers. He stood with

Teige before the huge hearth, and she pulled in a steadying breath and went to join him.

"You are ever more beautiful," he said softly, holding out his hands to her.

She took them, feeling the sword calluses upon his palms. His grip was strong, and reassuringly warm. As was his smile, and once again she was glad to be there at his side. Surely he was the most handsome mortal she'd ever seen.

"Are you ready?" Teige asked, and Conor nodded.

Maire drew in a breath and nodded, too.

"Good people of Castle Leamanagh!" Teige raised his voice so that all could hear. "We are here to witness the binding of Conor MacDonogh O'Brien, Lord of Leamanagh, with Maire Rua of the Oakwood."

The watchers let out a cheer, and even if some in the castle were not much pleased with their lord's choice, it was clear none would gainsay it. Even old Doireen's scowl had lifted, though she didn't go so far as to smile.

"Maire," Conor said, letting go of her hands, "I give you this ring to prove that my affections will remain constant and true, and so that you may bear proof of our binding."

He slipped a gold ring set with a large oval emerald onto her finger. It fit perfectly, the stone gleaming softly with a heart of forest green.

There was a moment of watchful silence, and she belatedly realized it was her turn.

"Conor." She pulled the heavy silver ring from the pocket of her gown. "I give you this ring in promise that my heart is truly bound to you, and no other, and that I will stand by your side as long as fate will allow."

And beyond, though the watching humans had no knowledge of the geas she'd agreed to in the Realm of Faerie. If she fulfilled her pledge, she and Conor would be reunited one day. It was the only thing that made the thought of his death bearable—for the longer she spent in his company, the more she leaned toward him like a flower seeking the light.

"Take hands," Teige said, once she'd placed the ring on Conor's finger.

They did, and Cara stepped forward to give Teige a length of ribbon braided in gold, red, and green.

"The O'Brien colors." Conor nodded to the banner above the hearth which depicted three pacing lions, gold and white, upon a field of scarlet. "And green for the grove."

As Teige wove the ribbon about their clasped hands, he spoke of vows and promises, the enduring strength of the O'Brien's, and wishes for prosperity.

"And children!" someone called as Teige tied off the ribbon.

"Indeed." Conor smiled widely, and Maire felt the joy shining from him. "Now, if you all don't mind, I'll be taking my new wife upstairs."

The cheer that followed them was more heartfelt than the first, ringing against the stone walls in a wash of goodwill that warmed Maire to the heart.

They navigated the stairs, Conor's right hand and Maire's left still bound together. She thought it a good omen that they did not stumble once along the way.

When they reached the upper hallway, he led her to his door, then paused and met her gaze.

"I don't know how such things are managed, in your realm," he said. "But among humans, once the bride and groom are wed it's customary to, er…"

He stared at her, as if hoping she'd give him the right words. She raised one brow, letting him dangle there like a fish upon a hook for a moment, then relented.

"I know what passes between man and maid. Indeed, I did not agree to marry you simply because of your quick wit and bravery."

"Well then." He pulled her to him, his mouth seeking hers.

She went willingly into his embrace. When their lips met, a dazzle of sensation coursed through her, a bright wind shaking her from the crown of her heat to the roots of her feet. She gripped his shoulder tightly to keep from being toppled, the muscular warmth of him keeping her steady against the storm.

When the kiss ended, he lifted his head with a slightly dazed look. "Had I known faerie maids had such magic in their kiss, I would have sought you out years ago."

"You would not have found me." She gave him a coy smile. "Fate brought us together at the appointed time. Though I would not have minded an earlier meeting, myself."

"We're here now, though, and I plan to make the most of it." He loosened the ribbons binding them, leaving them fluttering from her wrist. "Are you ready?"

Her heart beat quickly at the thought of touching him, skin to skin. Of letting her red hair fall down, curtaining their caresses. The fire in the hearth was nothing compared to the flame he set inside her.

"I am," she said softly.

He swept her up into his arms and carried her over the threshold to his bedroom.

The door shut firmly behind them, and it did not open until the next morning, much to everyone's satisfaction.

CHAPTER 7

THE NEXT SEVERAL weeks passed happily, despite Maire's occasional missteps concerning the ways of humans. She and Conor delighted in one another, and she found that not only was he bold and quick-witted, he had a tender side that made her feel as though she were the most precious thing in the world.

Despite the rain and cold, he rode out to the nearest grove and brought her an acorn.

"We'll plant it in the spring," he said, pressing it into her palm as she stood before the great hearth.

She closed her hand around it, smiling at him. The acorn was not the only promise of new life in the darkness of winter.

"The south side of the tower would be a good place for a sapling," she said.

"Ah, but I have other plans for that side." He slipped his arm about her waist, and she leaned into his embrace, breathing in the scent of his rain-washed hair.

When he didn't elaborate, she glanced up at him. "What plans might those be, Lord Mystery?"

He kissed the tip of her nose, then grew serious. "I think it's time to expand Leamanagh Castle. What do you think of a manor house filled with windows?"

She caught her breath, then took his hand and placed it over her belly. "It will be the perfect place to raise our family."

With a whoop, he caught her up and swung her about. The scattering of people in the hall smiled, then cheered when he shouted out the news that his new wife was with child.

Their lord's obvious joy with his choice of bride had done much to ease the distrust the people of Leamanagh had shown to Maire, and from that day forward, the babe-to-be sealed her place within the castle.

As Maire's belly began to swell, light returned to the world, pulling the days out and shortening the nights. One evening at supper, Conor announced it was time to begin raiding upon the English once more.

"Finally," Teige said. "I feared you'd gone soft over the winter, what with the distraction of your bed."

Conor laughed. "We'll find you a willing wife yet, never fear."

Maire glanced across the table at Cara, and raised her brows at the young woman. It hadn't escaped her notice that Cara's gaze followed Teige about the room, though he seemed oblivious to her interest. Maire had a plan to remedy his inattention, however—but first there was the matter of the raid.

"I'm coming with you," she said.

Conor turned to her with a frown. "But the babe—"

"Is scarcely sprouted in my belly. Do not deny me my promise, husband."

He let out a gusty sigh, but was wise enough not to argue any further.

And so it was that two nights later, Maire was dressed in a tunic and leggings, with a hardened leather chest piece and vambraces upon her arms. To her relief, Conor presented her with a bronze blade. She'd been prepared to ride out with only a small bow as a weapon, but having a sword at her side eased her mind.

"Can you use it, though?" Teige had asked as she buckled it on.

She shot him a wicked smile. "Shall we cross blades, so you can find out?"

The fair folk were light on their feet, quick, and unafraid to strike. Though she had not used a sword, she had watched the warriors train in the courtyard, and fixed the movements in her mind. Besides, she was stronger than most humans. She'd little doubt that she could wield the blade, especially if given an opportunity to practice.

The opportunity did not present itself that night, however. Their small band descended on an English interloper's fields and spirited away forty sheep and cows, with nary an outcry. Maire's only hurt was when the baby kicked for the first time as they were riding home, jabbing her uncomfortably beneath the ribs.

"Well done," Conor said when they'd penned the livestock up among Leamanagh's own sheep and cattle. "We'll ride out monthly until the weather turns. Or my son is born."

He winked at Maire as he helped her dismount.

She gave him a look. "And what makes you think it will be a son?"

"I just know it." He scooped her around the waist with one arm and kissed her heartily, then looked up and smiled at his foremost warrior. "And we will name him Teige."

Fall came, and with it the rains and a blue-eyed baby boy they named Teige, as promised. By that time, Maire's subtle, and not-so-subtle, prompting had resulted in the warrior Teige's own handfasting to Cara.

Work had begun on the manor house. As promised, it bore a multitude of windows. And by autumn, the little acorn Conor had planted by the east wall had sent out a strong shoot.

One year passed from the day Maire had come to the human world to marry her bold and handsome lord, and they were as happy as ever. Then another year came, and a third, with a brother for Teige. Maire continued to ride out with her husband against the English, and soon tales of her ferocity began to circulate throughout the countryside. Maire Rua they called her, both for her flame-red hair and her ferocity in battle. Four years flew past, bringing another son, then five, and Conor sustained a wound in battle that struck Maire to the core with fear. She tended him night and day, desperate not to lose her beloved.

At midnight, she went down to the oak sapling and wept bitterly. *Not now*, she pleaded with any spirit who might listen. *Not so soon.*

The night wind blew, unheeding, and the stars gave her no answers.

But as dawn put a blush into the sky's cheek, Conor's fever broke and he was able to drink a bit of broth. The worst was over.

CHAPTER 8

TWELVE YEARS ON, and Maire and Conor had eight children shrieking and running about the upper halls of the manor house. The oak tree had grown, waiting patiently beside the stone wall of the old tower. Each season it rose higher, bearing the cold wind off the plain and the turning of each year from dark to light and back again.

The prospect of her beloved's death had receded far from the oak-maiden's mind, for as time passed she'd become more human than faerie. Her days were taken up with the running of the household and the castle, the mothering of eight children, and carving out a bit of time for herself and Conor to steal away together—whether it was a long ride out upon the Burren, or a quick tumble with the door barred.

But their contentment was not to last.

"Bad news," Conor said one afternoon, coming in from meeting with the local landholders.

Maire rose from her seat in the main parlor, where she'd been telling stories to the younger children.

"Run off, now," she said, kissing Honora's cheek and

ruffling Murrough's hair. "And take your younger sisters with you."

They went, Murrough sending a questioning look at his father, who patted him on one shoulder. When the four children were gone, Maire went and took her husband's hands, noting the lines of worry bracketing his mouth.

"What is it?" she asked, a cold dart of fear piercing her chest.

"Ireton's marching again," he said grimly.

Maire shivered, gripping her husband tightly. The previous year, Cromwell's army had brought terrible suffering and death to the eastern part of Ireland, and especially to Limerick, the last fortified bastion of those who refused to accept English rule. Though the city had at last surrendered to General Ireton, he'd withdrawn in the face of one of the bleakest winters the country had known.

Now, though, it seemed he was back to crush the city beneath his boot.

"Surely we're safe here," she said.

Leamanagh was enough off the main route. Surely the English wouldn't attack?

"We might be safe," Conor said. "But what of Ennis, of Shannon, and especially what of Limerick? The city cannot withstand another invasion. I'm taking my warriors and meeting up with the other lords and their men. We'll stop Ireton at the Pass of Inchicronan."

In the far, far distance, Maire heard a banshee's wail.

"No," she said softly, trying to keep her voice steady. "Please, stay here with me."

"I cannot," he said simply.

She clutched at his shoulders, pressed kisses upon his lips, his cheeks, his hair, but he would not be turned from his path.

"You must let me go," he said, giving her a last, lingering kiss and then stepping back. "I could not face myself each day if I sat idly by and did nothing to try and stop this monster from descending upon our people."

"Even if…" She drew in a ragged breath. "Even if it meant your doom?"

"Even then." He met her gaze. "I have lived as a man of honor and as a warrior, and I shall die the same, if need be."

"Then take me with you."

He shook his head. "It's too dangerous. And we cannot leave our children with neither a father nor a mother."

"I'd be safe," she pleaded. "I swear it, by the sun and moon. By the oak grove."

"Yet I'd still fear for you at every clash of blade. I love you, Maire, my heart, but your presence at this battle would cloud my thoughts and slow my sword. Even as I must go, you must stay here and await my return. I will come back to you. I promise."

Tears spilled from her eyes, running hot and reckless down her cheeks, but she knew she could not change his mind. And perhaps his promise would hold true. She clung to the thought. Perhaps he would return to her, after all.

"When do you ride?" she whispered at last.

"Tomorrow, at dawn."

That night, neither of them slept, but passed the dark hours in one another's arms, learning and relearning the ways their bodies fit together. Their kisses were filled with urgency, and heat, and at last, the bittersweet salt of their sorrow.

CHAPTER 9

MAIRE WATCHED the men ride off over the limestone plain. Her children had bade their father sleepy farewells and gone back to the warmth of their beds, but she lingered outside Leamanagh as the dark shapes of the mounted warriors disappeared into the dawn.

"Come, have some tea and bread," Cara coaxed, taking Maire's arm.

Her voice was heavy, too, for Teige had ridden away at Conor's side.

"I'll come, soon," Maire said, her gaze still focused on the empty horizon.

Ever a true friend, Cara gave her a brief embrace and withdrew back into the manor. In the silence, Maire took a deep breath, then rounded the side of the old tower to where the oak tree stood. In the dozen years since Conor had planted it for her, it had grown tall and strong. The branches reached over her head now, and the new leaves rustled softly, though there was no wind.

Maire placed her hand against the rough bark. For a

moment, she wished with all her might for the door to open. Wished she could step back into the Realm of Faerie and let the weight of her mortal heart go, for it was too heavy a burden for her to bear.

But the door did not appear, as she knew it would not.

All that was left to her was the comfort of the mortal world: a house filled with light, a friend waiting with a cup of tea, her dear and devilish children. And the dreadful sword of waiting poised over her head.

The day crept by, agonizingly slow. Morning creaked into midday, and then into afternoon. Maire tried to distract herself with the household tasks, with meals and cleaning and the company of her children.

Then the blade fell.

Maire cried aloud, feeling the blow to her own chest as Conor took his mortal wound. Sobbing, she fell to her knees. The grief tore her in two, rending her heart, her breath, blinding her.

I never should have loved him, her heart wailed. *I cannot bear his passing.*

"What is it?" Cara knelt beside her and took her shoulders.

Maire could not speak, merely shook her head and squeezed her eyes shut, willing the agony to cease. She rocked back and forth, fingers clenched in her skirts.

"Breathe," Cara murmured, pulling her close.

Maire took a long, ragged breath, then began to weep as though she would never stop.

At long last, her grief was spent. Her eyes felt sore, her chest scoured. The tears would return, she knew, but for now she was able to thank Cara. Was able to rise shakily to her feet and seek the shelter of her bed.

The sheets still smelled of Conor, and her heart broke anew.

Teige and the other men returned well after dark, bearing Conor.

"He still lives," the warrior said when Maire met them at the gate. "Barely."

She nodded. Her husband would not see the dawn, but she could look upon his beloved face once more.

"Bring him upstairs, to the guest room."

It would not matter to Conor, but if he died in their bed, she would never be able to sleep there again, or recall all the laughter and sweetness they'd shared.

They laid him gently down, then withdrew to leave Maire with her dying husband. The wound upon his chest could not be tended to; he'd lost too much blood, and the rasp of his breathing signaled he would not linger long in the mortal world.

"My love." Maire smoothed the grey-shot dark hair from his forehead. "Listen to me."

To her astonishment, his eyelids fluttered and he opened his eyes. She looked into those stormy blue depths, and forced herself to be strong.

"You must leave me now," she said. "But the Realm of Faerie awaits, my bold warrior. I will come to you there, as soon as my geas is fulfilled. We will be together again. I promise."

She saw a spark of understanding in his eyes. Then he closed them, and breathed his last,

"Wait for me," she whispered.

Then bent over his lifeless body and let sorrow overwhelm her once more. Her only solace was that Conor was now in the Realm. She would see him again, though years would pass in the mortal world.

An eternity, her heart whispered. But she would bear it.

The day after Conor's funeral, Maire pulled the tatters of her strength about her, and told the people of the castle that she would seek a new husband.

"The English will take Leamanagh, unless I am wed," she said, which was true enough.

General Ireton had marked Conor's rebellion, and was eager to seize the castle and its lands for his own people. The only way she could stave off the English and keep her family from being cast out was to find a new lord for Leamanagh.

Accordingly, she dressed in her finest gown of silver and blue and rode to Limerick to find herself a new husband from among the English. For a year and a day, if she could make him agree to it. And if not, he would bring his doom upon himself.

Two days later, she returned to Leamanagh with Captain John Cooper, who was brave and foolhardy enough to agree to her terms.

"There will be no children," she told him. "And my people have little love for anyone serving in Ireton's army. But if you will marry me for a year and a day, I will give you a fat purse of gold when you depart."

Most of the year passed in a shroud of sorrow, but John

Cooper made her smile from time to time, and when the time had ended, he kissed her hand and wished her well.

One over with, she thought as she stood at the top of the old tower and watched him ride away. Twenty-four more to endure.

CHAPTER 10

A DOZEN YEARS PASSED, along with a dozen more husbands. Maire's children were her one joy, and she thanked all the powers that be that she'd been so blessed. As for the marriage bed, Maire became hardened to the terms of her geas, though her longing for Conor never ceased. At night she dreamed of him, and by day the echo of his laughter followed her about the manor house.

Her children grew up, headstrong and fair, and sought lives for themselves outside of Leamanagh's bounds. Her eldest son moved the family seat to Castle Dromoland, nearer to Limerick. Though he entreated his mother to join him there, she refused. Her punishment must be carried out at Leamanagh.

It went well enough, until her thirteenth husband.

"I will not leave," he said, after a year and a day had passed.

"You must," Maire pleaded.

He folded his arms and glanced about the opulent lord's suite of Leamanagh. "I like it here very well. Why should I seek another home?"

"Because to stay will spell your doom," she said, despairing.

"I don't believe you."

A darkness moved over the room, and a moment later the banshee Aibell stood there. Her eyes were black hollows, and her mouth stretched in an evil smile.

"Perhaps you will believe *me*," she said.

Before he could utter another word, the banshee rushed toward him, hands outstretched. He stumbled back, into the high window.

The shatter of glass mingled with his scream as he fell.

Aghast, Maire stared at Aibell. "You have no right!"

"I have every right," The banshee lifted a long, bony finger. "Best choose your temporary husbands with more care, Maire Rua. Else I'll be visiting you more often."

The sound of people in the hallway made them both glance at the door. When Maire looked back into the room, Aibell was gone.

"Maire!" Cara burst through the door. "What happened?"

"I...he stumbled," she said, spreading her hands. "Before I knew it, he was gone."

Cara pulled her into an embrace, but Maire saw the glances exchanged by the others. Without Conor there to champion her, without the ability to explain her geas, the tide of suspicion was beginning to turn against her.

Twelve more years passed. The oak tree outside the old tower waited, branches reaching toward the sky, and at last Maire wed her twenty-fifth husband.

It was a difficult pairing—Maire had married Tormond in

haste, eager to finish her geas, and had not chosen as well as perhaps she should. Six months into the union, he told her he was leaving.

"You cannot," she said. "You promised."

"I find I don't like having a wife that cares not for me," he said. "I'd prefer to seek another."

"Wait," she said, following him down the wide stairs of the manor house. "Another sixmonth and a day, and you can do as you please, with a fat purse of gold, besides."

He pushed her away when she reached for him. "I'd rather have my freedom than your accursed goin."

"You will die," she said, desperation edging her voice.

"Empty threats." He laughed at her and pulled open the door. "Goodbye, Maire Rua. I wish you an unpleasant future."

Cold rain spattered the threshold, a reminder that the year was near to turning.

"Don't go," she cried. She did not love the man, but she'd seen enough death.

Only last year, the warrior Teige had stepped through the veil, leaving Cara to grieve alone. Later, she'd moved away to Ennis to live with her daughters. Maire still felt her loss keenly, especially when the people of Leamanagh and the nearby village cast wary glances at her and whispered of her evil ways.

"There's my mount," Tormond said, striding out into the rain-lashed night toward a sleek black horse.

Heart clenching, Maire rushed after him.

"Wait!" she cried, grabbing his arm. "That is no mortal horse."

It was a kelpie, an unseelie creature that would bind a rider to its back and bear them to their doom. The black gleam of its coat was as dark as midnight, and an eerie wind tousled its mane.

Too late. Tormond wrenched away from her and swung up upon the horse.

"Farewell." He scowled down at her. "I hope never to see you again."

The kelpie charged away, and with a heavy heart she watched it go. She'd no doubt it would bear Tormond over the cliffs and straight into the gnashing teeth of the sea. But there was nothing she could do to avert his fate.

Still, she stood in the cold, letting the rain drench her hair and cloak, and lamenting her failure.

You are free, now, her heart whispered. *Your geas is complete.*

The knowledge was an ember of warmth in her chest. Surely Conor awaited her there, in the Realm of Faerie. She turned back to the house. She'd write letters of farewell to her children and to Cara, say goodbye to the rooms where she'd spent her mortal happiness. And then she would go.

CHAPTER 11

"Mistress!" One of the servants burst into her chamber while Maire was sealing up the last letter, this one addressed to Cara.

"What is it?" She rose, alarmed by the fearful expression on his face.

"They're coming for you," he said. "With torches and blades."

"Who is coming?" Already she was reaching for her cloak. "And why?"

"The villagers. They say you've murdered Tormond—killed all your husbands, in fact. They mean to kill you."

She swallowed the rusty taste of fear. "Make sure these letters are delivered."

"Where are you going?" He held out his hand to stop her, but Maire brushed past.

"Away," she said, hoping it wasn't too late.

When she stepped out of Leamanagh, an ugly crowd was gathering at the gates.

"There she is!" someone shouted.

"Catch her!"

Maire whirled and dashed for the tower. She must reach the oak.

The crack of the gates giving way was loud in the night, the cries of her pursuers like the shrill baying of the Wild Hunt after their quarry. She rounded the corner, the breath rasping in her throat, and ran for the shelter of the tree.

"Let me in!" she cried, pressing her hands upon the rough bark.

The oak tree shook, but no doorway into the Realm of Faerie appeared. She pressed her body against the tree, her cheek scraping the bark.

"My promise is fulfilled," she said, desperation in her voice. "Please, open."

No dark door appeared within the trunk, no sound of harp or whisper of enchanted wind. She was trapped within the mortal world, with her death looming.

The bloodthirsty crowd rounded the corner, and Maire fell to her knees in despair.

"Conor," she whispered.

As if his name were a key, an opening appeared in the nubbled bark, a crack that widened until, at last, the way to Faerie lay before her.

Maire tumbled inside, feeling the tug upon her cloak as her pursuers tried to haul her back. The oak closed with a crack of wood against wood, catching her cloak and holding it fast.

She didn't care, however, for she lay upon the soft emerald moss of the Realm. The air was soft, and overhead a handful of stars shimmered in the endless sky.

She was home.

Slowly, she sat up, her chest filled with so much lightness that she thought she might float away. She unfastened her cloak and rose, abandoning the mortal garment. With a thought, she turned her woolen dress to gossamer silk. Her braids unwound, her scarlet hair falling free about her face.

"So, ye've returned." Aibell's voice was harsh against the quiet of the Dusklands.

Maire turned to see the banshee clad in black tatters, standing beside the oak. For moment, fear smote her. Had Aibell had come to tell her Conor was not there?

No, such a thing could not be. Maire had fulfilled the terms of the bargain.

"I'm here to claim my true love," she said.

"And so you shall." Aibell gestured, and a heartbeat later Conor came striding over the mossy hill.

Mortal tears pricked Maire's eyes, and she ran toward him, even as he shouted her name and rushed to meet her. They embraced tightly, Conor pressing kisses on her forehead, her cheeks, her lips.

"You waited," she said, when she could catch her breath.

"Of course. I would wait for you forever, my love." His gaze met hers, deep and true, the color of a summer storm. "But I'm glad it was not too long."

She nodded, though it had been much longer for her—an eternity of yearning.

Over now.

Her heart was as free as a swallow, dipping lightly over the land, as clear as the moonlight shining overhead.

"We have all the time we need, now," she said, twining her fingers in his.

"Yes." He smiled at her, the maiden who had stolen his heart, who had saved his life.

Hand in hand, they strode beneath the trees, the whispering oaks of Faerie guarding their secrets forever.

~*~

HEART OF THE FOREST

CHAPTER 1

PRINCE KENTRY of Raine leaned low over his mount's lathered neck, his heartbeat echoing the thud of his horse's hooves, until he was a single pulse of purpose.

Ride. Hunt. He must capture the impossible creature fleeing before him—the fable he'd only half-believed, until the force of his need propelled him into the treacherous reaches of the forest.

Ahead, his quarry flickered through the trees in full, leaping flight. Flashes of sunlight limned the wide crown of its antlers, struck silver from its hide.

The White Hart.

One handed, Kent reached for the net slung across the pommel of his saddle. So close…

The creature veered off with a sudden burst of speed as the dark lacing of cedar branches opened to a clearing. Kent spurred his horse after it. The sharp scent of crushed ferns hung in the air as the pale shape of the stag vaulted back into the Darkwood's embrace.

Undaunted, he followed.

"Kentry! Prince!"

"Wait!"

The shouts of his companions faded as he reentered the cool shadows beneath the trees. The White Hart fled along a game trail barely wide enough for Kent's mount to follow. Bushes raked at his sides and he was forced to duck to avoid low-hanging boughs. The wet, musty smell of upturned loam hung in the air.

Faster. Faster.

Surely he was closing the distance. Behind him, the mournful cry of a hunting horn sounded, as faint as a mother's call to her wayward child.

A red-breasted bird fluttered, startled, past his head. Shafts of sun speared through the evergreens, striking down like solid columns through the dark branches. Pale yellow flowers nodded on graceful stems, blurring past so quickly he scarcely glimpsed them. The path swerved around a bush laden with translucent red berries tucked among coin-shaped leaves.

Other than the rasp of his breathing, the silence pressed down. His horse's hoof beats were muffled by the carpet of cedar needles strewn over emerald moss. The birds had all stopped singing. No more shouts sounded behind him.

It was only him, his gelding, and the glowing White Hart leading him into the depths of the forest.

When he'd announced his intention to ride into the Darkwood in search of the fabled beast, his family had thought him mad. The dinner conversation had halted while his older brothers exchanged skeptical looks across the long, candle-bedecked dining hall of the palace.

"Certainly not," his mother had said.

His father, the king, had cleared his throat and asked Kent to present himself in the royal parlor after supper.

The parlor, at least, was cozier than the formal throne room. The late evening light scattered shadows over the ornate Parnesian carpets, and the room smelled pleasantly of leather and his mother's rose perfume. Despite this, Kent stood uncomfortably, stance wide, hands clasped behind his back as he faced his parents.

"Don't go," his mother begged him. "I know your heart is sore, but once your brother is married, surely it will mend."

Kent shook his head, sending a lock of overlong dark hair into his eyes. He swiped it out of his face impatiently. "I will always love Maired, and seeing her as the future queen will only twist the blade in my heart. Every single day."

"But is this mad quest necessary?" His father rocked forward onto the balls of his feet. "I know you're young and hot-headed, much like myself at your age"—he gave a rueful chuckle, and the queen smiled at him—"but there are other ways you might cool your emotions. You've often expressed a desire to see more of the world. We could appoint you as our ambassador to the Fiorland court. Or to a post in Caliss, if that doesn't suit."

"I want neither of those things," Kent said, hating the roughness of his voice. He *had* wanted them, before love had submerged him in a ferocious storm—but now it was too late. "The stories say that, once captured, the White Hart will grant your heart's desire."

His mother's delicately arched brows rose. "And what of your brother's desire? He cares deeply for Maired, too. What kind of man would steal away the future king's bride and cast such melancholy over the throne of Raine?"

Kent made a slashing motion with his hand. "Both of you are in excellent health. Ian won't take the throne for years. He'll have plenty of time to find another wife."

Still, he couldn't help the curdling suspicion that they were right. Although he'd tried to tell himself that Maired had agreed to marry his brother only because he was to be king, Kent couldn't deny that she and Ian shared a deep affection.

Not as deep as Kent's own hot and piercing love, of course. It had shattered him when Maired had, ever-so-gently, told him that Ian had proposed—and that she'd accepted.

"Surely the White Hart, being a creature of Raine, wouldn't do anything to endanger the kingdom," Kent said.

"Hm." The king regarded him steadily. "Do recall, the Darkwood is older than the kingdom, and full of strangeness. There's a reason no one dwells close to the forest's edges."

"Well, perhaps we should!" Kent retorted. "It's time to stop being so afraid of a collection of trees."

"That 'collection of trees,' as you term it, spreads across half the country." His father's tone dipped with disappointment. "It's teeming with bear and wolves, not to mention other creatures—if the tales can be believed. And might I point out that if you're going after the White Hart, you can't dismiss the darker things rumored to lurk in the forest."

Kent shifted impatiently. Surely his need was great enough that he would prevail. After all, if the burning in his brain scarcely allowed him to sleep, it would certainly guide him to the creature that could grant his greatest wish.

"In any case," he said, "I'm going into the Darkwood. The huntsmaster has agreed to let me bring two of his best trackers and their hounds."

"But you must have other companions!" The queen clasped

her hands in agitation. "What if you become lost in the forest?"

Kent heaved a sigh. He'd anticipated his mother's concern, however, and was prepared for this objection.

"Lord Carkin and Cousin Sean will accompany me." He couldn't leave his oldest friend behind, and Sean had a talent for inviting himself along, whether he was wanted or not.

A touch of relief smoothed his mother's expression. "At least your cousin can be depended upon."

"Then it's settled," Kent said. "I'll ride out in the morning."

He hadn't been able to bear the thought of seeing Maired again. Since the announcement of her engagement, even the briefest encounter with her in the palace corridors had set a torch to his lungs.

And so, before the summer sun had dispelled the misty dawn air, Kent and his companions rode out. It was a long day's journey from Meriton to the edge of the Darkwood, and though he'd wanted to begin the hunt that evening, Cousin Sean had persuaded him to make camp and wait until daybreak.

For the next three days they'd searched fruitlessly for signs of their quarry, until one of the hounds had finally caught a scent. Baying joyously, it had led them deeper into the forest. At last Kent had glimpsed the silvery stag that was his prize.

Now, the White Hart bounded before him, leaping gracefully down a fern-carpeted slope. Kent followed, blessing his surefooted mount, aptly named Nimble. He set one hand to the net he carried. Although his bow was slung across his back, his goal was to snare the stag, not kill it.

The White Hart burst into a meadow, Kent at its heels. He grabbed the net and bent lower over his horse's neck. Closer.

Closer. He could hear the beast snorting for breath, see the white of its eye and smell its sweet, wild odor.

In the corner of Kent's vision, he glimpsed a tall stone, sparkling eerily—but he had no time to pause. He readied the net, lifting it overhead…

The White Hart glowed beneath the encroaching darkness of the trees, the sunlight gone between one breath and the next. Kent's mount faltered. His throw missed, the net capturing nothing but a bush covered in glowing purple flowers.

The pale form of the stag slipped between the enormous tree trunks and was gone.

Heart pounding, Kent drew Nimble to a stop. He leaned down and gathered up his net, inhaling the richness of loam and cedar, and then took stock of his surroundings.

Between one heartbeat and the next, the Darkwood had transformed, growing fierce and magical. Strange blooms glowed with their own radiance beneath the fronded branches of the evergreens that now towered high above him, blocking all the light.

He squinted up, dismayed to see a huge golden moon floating in a dark sky brushed with unrecognizable stars. And was that another moon, trailing behind its brighter sister?

Where, by all the seas, was he?

Movement again, between the trees. For an instant the shape of the silver deer was outlined against the green-black shadows. Casting aside his confusion, Kent urged his mount forward. This time, he vowed, the White Hart would not escape.

CHAPTER 2

Fanyaleth Lasgalen woke with a start from her moss-cradled sleep. The tall cedars of the forest waved above her in an invisible breeze and she stared up at them from the green depths of her ferny bower. Something had echoed through her dreams—a strange, mournful call, a shimmer of magic…

Sitting, she lifted her palm and called a blue sphere of foxfire, then sent it to hover overhead. She'd been wandering the Erynvorn for three days, and was wary of encountering the strange creatures said to roam the depths of the forest. But her light revealed nothing dangerous—no insidious spawn of the Void that could only be vanquished by the power of a warrior-mage. No red-eyed dire wolves skulking in the underbrush, no scaled drakes or poison-fanged basilisks lurking, ready to pounce.

Not that Fanya was sure the latter creatures existed, beyond the tales told to Dark Elf children to warn them to approach the Erynvorn with caution. If at all.

She'd had no choice, however. The prophecy spoken at her birth had commanded her to enter the dark bastion of the forest on the doublemoon after her seventeenth birthday. Since ignoring the Oracles was a sure path to madness and ruin, here she was, sleeping in the bracken, picking twigs from her long silver hair, and spending her days foraging for berries and mushrooms.

That shiver went through the air again, and Fanya rose, half crouching beneath the huge moss-covered log that had given her shelter. She dismissed her foxfire and took up her bow, which she'd laid close to hand. Quickly, she drew a sharp-tipped arrow from her quiver.

Something was coming toward her through the trees. Silver flashed, and she glimpsed a regal set of antlers. Then the creature was upon her, its graceful form soaring over her hiding place with a mighty leap.

As the White Hart sailed past, it sent her a look from one dark, liquid eye, as though it were trying to warn her. She caught her breath at its majesty, the luminous magic it trailed.

Then it was gone, and whatever was crashing through the underbrush after it burst through the trees. A figure on horseback, sword at his side, net in his hand. She hesitated a moment—but no one with pure intent would hunt the White Hart.

Fanya raised her bow, aiming for the rider's shoulder. She wanted to wound, not kill.

Her arrow flew—just as his net descended over her, fouling her bow and pulling her arms against her sides with its weight. A cry of pain made her smile grimly, even as she twisted within the net. She might be snared, but her arrow had met its mark.

"Cruel beast," the rider said, his words oddly accented. "How dare you wound me?"

He brought his mount to stop in front of her and slid down one-handed, clutching the arrow shaft protruding from the meat of his upper arm. Not quite what Fanya had intended, but close enough.

"How dare *you* hunt the White Hart?" she replied hotly. "It is a sacred creature."

"But I've caught you, despite that." The hunter grinned, though his smile turned to a grimace of pain as he leaned forward. "Now you owe me my heart's desire."

Belatedly, Fanya realized she was facing a mortal man. His oddly short hair should have alerted her, his strange human eyes and round-tipped ears—just as in the tales her people told. It had been a long time since a human had been spotted in the Erynvorn, however. Clearly, the White Hart had brought him.

"Let me go," she said, forcing one elbow through the net. Given time, she'd be able to free herself, but it would be much easier if he'd simply remove it.

"Not until you grant my wish." Despite his bold words, he ended with a small grunt of pain.

She narrowed her eyes. "Free me, and I'll pull my arrow from your arm and dress the wound."

He glanced down at the protruding shaft, then back at her. "Although that's a pressing need, it's not my heart's desire."

"I'd think not bleeding to death on the forest floor would be anyone's wish."

"The injury's not that bad." He sent her a smile, his jaw clenched in obvious pain.

"Are all humans so foolishly stubborn? I nearly pierced your arm straight through." She impatiently shrugged at the net covering her. "Release me, and I'll help you."

"You won't run?"

She glanced at his mount, which stood patiently behind him. "You'd catch me again easily enough."

It wasn't *quite* true—he was a stranger to the forest, and she could possibly find a hole to hide in, or scale one of the huge hemlocks and disappear among the feathery treetops. But beyond the fact that she wouldn't relish being chased through the Erynvorn, she had injured him, and could not leave him to wander.

Not to mention that the smell of his blood could call other, darker things out of the depths of the forest to menace them both.

"I'd only catch you if didn't transform again," he said tersely.

Fanya blinked at him, belatedly realizing he thought *she* was the White Hart. Despite being the wrong gender. Still, it seemed to her advantage to say nothing and let him believe she was, indeed, that powerful, enchanted creature.

"Free me, and I will not flee from you," she said. "I promise—and my kind do not break our word."

He nodded, once, then stepped forward, fingers still clenched around the arrow buried in his arm. At least he was wise enough not to wrench at it. The barbed head would tear through his flesh if he tried to pull it out, making the wound far worse.

"Crouch down," he said as he awkwardly tried to pull the net off of her, one-handed.

Her shoulders tensed and she forced herself to breathe deeply of the rich loam as she went to her knees. Should this human try to attack her again, she had the knife at her belt—and her magic, although she'd never been taught the dangerous combat runes her people traditionally used in battle.

An oversight she would most certainly remedy as soon as she returned to the Moonflower Court.

The human had peeled away half the net when a long, wavering howl shivered through the forest. Fanya struggled out of the rest of the strands, fear spiking her blood while the human's horse danced backward a few steps, eyes rolling in fright.

"What was that?" he asked, plucking at the net still wrapped about her bow.

"Direwolf. Hold still." She stepped forward, nostrils flaring at the strange, spicy scent of him. But this was no time for distraction, no matter how strange it was to stand so close to a human.

With quick, efficient movements, she tore a larger hole in the arm of his shirt around the protruding arrow. Taking hold of the shaft in both hands, she snapped it, removing the fletched end. He winced at the movement. Then, before he could protest, she drove the arrow point through the rest of his arm and out the other side. He made a strangled sound of agony, but, impressively, didn't cry out, even though the pain doubled him over for a moment.

She tucked her broken, bloody arrow back into her quiver, then placed her hands on either side of his arm and murmured a quick rune of healing to staunch the blood. Wide-eyed, he turned to look at her. Their gazes caught, and she blinked at his nearness.

"You *are* magic," he whispered.

Then the wolf howled once more, and Fanya jerked away.

"It's only a minor rune," she said. "But it will help until we reach a true healer."

She turned and plucked her bow free of the net, which he quickly folded away.

"And where will we find one of those?" He turned and scanned the forest.

"Not here—and we should go." Though a part of her might wish to, she couldn't abandon him in the Erynvorn. Even though he was no longer bleeding, he was still wounded. And though she wasn't pleased at the fact that prophecy had thrust a human into her life, there was no arguing with fate.

He turned to his horse, lifted his hands to the saddle, then let out a grunt of pain.

"You're not healed," she said. "Only slightly mended. You must favor your arm."

He gave her a tight nod and, face pale, mounted. As soon as he was settled, she set her hand on the horse's side, accustoming the animal to her touch.

"I will ride with you," she said. Then, before he could protest, she murmured a quick feather-light rune and leapt up behind him.

His mount whuffled softly, but didn't object to her presence on its back.

"Oh." The human turned to look at her over his shoulder. "I thought you might…"

"I told you I would not transform," she said—which was not a *complete* falsehood. She couldn't turn herself into a white deer, even if she wanted to. None of her people could change their forms, no matter what this mortal man seemed to think.

His eyebrows drew together in question, but before he could voice any objection, she prodded the horse into motion.

Quickly, he swiveled to face forward and guide his mount around the mossy hollow beneath the log where she'd taken shelter.

"That way." She pointed to the left, trying to ignore the heat of him seated before her, the musky, not-unpleasant mortal scent drifting from his shorn hair.

"How far are we going?"

It was a good question. She frowned, thinking. Certainly not all the way to Moonflower, which was a journey of nearly two doublemoons. No, they'd have to make for one of the outer courts. Nightshade was the closest, if she wasn't mistaken.

"Some distance," she finally answered. "We'll have to sleep in the forest tonight."

She would set wards, of course.

And, somehow, once he was healed, they must determine how to send him back to the mortal realm. But that was a powerful magic indeed, and one she had no hope of performing on her own.

CHAPTER 3

Following the maiden's directions, Kent guided his horse between the massive evergreens and around great tangles of briars studded with dark purple berries. The wound in his arm pulsed unpleasantly, but not as painfully as it ought to, given the nature of the injury. He supposed he ought to be grateful that the deer-maiden had tended to it, even though she'd been the one to wound him in the first place.

He hadn't anticipated that she'd be armed, or quite so combative in nature. Some of the tales he'd discovered in the palace library had mentioned that the White Hart, once captured, might turn into a silver-haired maiden. He'd been prepared for that possibility, although the stories differed on whether or not she was a princess or simply an enchanted creature.

None of them had mentioned that she carried a bow fitted with wickedly pointed arrows and possessed a tongue nearly as sharp.

"Do you have a name?" he asked.

Despite her assurances, he couldn't decide if she were

truthful in nature. If only he could see her face when she answered, so he might study her pale, mist-blue eyes for the flicker of a lie. Her delicate features were mostly human, though her cheekbones were sharper, and he'd noticed the pointed tips of her ears peeking out from the pale fall of her hair.

"Of course I have a name." She sounded offended by his question, though she didn't offer him an answer.

Kent shook his head. He'd never imagined a deer to be quite so cross in nature. Though he supposed any creature would be irritated by being chased down and captured.

"I am Prince Kentry Larnach of the Kingdom of Raine," he said, belatedly realizing how pompous his title sounded, spoken into the hushed depths of the forest. There was no need for such ceremony here. "But Kent will do."

The maiden at his back was quiet for a moment, as if weighing her words.

"You may call me Fanya," she finally said.

"Are you a princess?"

She let out a soft snort of amusement, her breath briefly warming the back of his neck. "Do such things matter greatly to mortals?"

"It matters who governs a kingdom, who the ruling family is." He frowned, though she couldn't see it.

"Then are you destined to rule some mortal realm?"

"No," he said shortly, wishing he hadn't started the conversation.

Better to have a silent deer-maiden at his back than these sharp-edged questions prodding at his old pain.

At least the wolves were no longer howling in the distance.

"Is that your heart's desire, then?" she asked. "To rule a kingdom?"

"Not necessarily. It isn't what drove me to seek you out, if that's what you mean."

Another quiet sound of disbelief at his back. "Then what did?"

He shot an annoyed glance over his shoulder, catching a glimpse of her shimmering hair and one pointed ear.

"Aren't you supposed to know such things?" he demanded. "You're a creature of magic and fable, after all."

She didn't reply immediately, and Kent concentrated on guiding his mount around a fallen tree, its roots a twisted snarl above a moss-filled depression.

"Even the most magical being cannot read a heart that does not know its own way," she said at last.

"I know what I want." He kept his voice low and controlled, though he wanted to shout the words. Wanted to yell his frustration into the forest until the very trees shook with the depth of his longing.

"Hm," the maiden said.

The doubt in that single syllable almost made him leap from his horse and confront her, force her to immediately grant his wish. Of *course* he knew what he wanted! For Maired to love him back, as fiercely as he loved her.

But he was wounded, as his aching arm reminded him. And even though the howls of the wolves had faded, his demands could wait until they made camp.

"You didn't answer my question," he said, trying to turn the tables.

"Did I not?" Her voice was lightly amused. "You have so many, it's difficult to keep track."

He clenched his jaw, beating back annoyance. This wasn't how he'd envisioned the triumphant end of his hunt—wounded, and burdened with a strange maiden who refused to grant his wish and instead seemed to take a great deal of satisfaction in needling him.

And yet, he was familiar enough with hiding his own pain behind a veneer of mockery that he recognized that Fanya was doing the same. Why else would she jab him with her questions if not to deflect his own queries in return?

"So," he said, drawing his own conclusions, "you *are* a princess, after all."

He felt her go still behind him.

"Can an enchanted deer even *be* a princess?" she asked, though the amusement in her voice sounded forced. "It seems unlikely. Wouldn't my circlet tangle in my antlers? Which item, might I point out, I'm not wearing."

"Just because you don't currently have a crown atop your head doesn't mean you're not entitled to wear one. My question stands."

She blew out an annoyed breath, and a small, grim smile crossed his face. Pursuing the truth from her was almost as enjoyable as running his silver-coated quarry to ground, and a welcome distraction from the sharp throbbing in his arm. He suspected he would win this battle of words, too.

"We have no kingdoms, here," she said.

A slippery answer, but he was learning to hear what she left unsaid.

"Then what *do* you have?"

She shifted behind him and went silent for several moment. He was opening his mouth to ask her again, when she replied, "We have courts."

His brows lifted. Courts, but not kingdoms? It seemed a small distinction. "And what court do you hail from, Lady Fanya?"

"Moonflower."

She hadn't challenged his use of *lady*—which he guessed meant she was used to the title. And that he was wearing her down.

"Is that where we're going, to finish tending my injury?"

"No. That court is too far. We're headed to Nightshade."

"That sounds…ominous."

As if underscoring his words, a bird flashed from the underbrush. The blue of its startled wings matched the memory of the daylit skies of Raine.

"Nightshade might be one of the outer courts, but it's not entirely unpolished," Fanya said. "There's no cause for alarm."

"Perhaps." He would make his own determination once they reached the court. "Will we make camp soon? Your two moons are very pretty, but I'd rather travel by daylight."

"Daylight?"

He made an impatient gesture, then winced as it jarred his wounded arm. "When does the sun rise, here in your land?"

"If you mean a great glowing sphere of fire burning across the sky, we do not have a sun."

"No sun?" For the first time a wisp of fear wreathed around his heart. How far had the White Hart led him from the mortal world? And would she send him back, once his wish was granted?

Surely she must.

Yet other tales tickled his memory, of humans trapped for decades—centuries even—in a mystical land where time moved differently, if it existed at all. Enthralled by fey creatures, like the one who rode at his back. Ensorcelled until they forgot what it was to be mortal.

No. Such a fate was not for him. He would return to Raine, where Maired would be waiting with open arms, her eyes alight with a smile meant only for him.

And then what? a treacherous part of him whispered. Would he truly remain at the palace in Meriton, after stealing away his brother's fiancée? That could only result in bitter unhappiness, for all involved.

Well then, he and Maired would travel, as he'd always dreamed—visiting Fiorland in the summer, and Parnese in the winter. When they were ready, they'd find a pleasant place to settle down and raise a family.

Far from their own families…

Enough. Kent reined his thoughts back to his current predicament—injured and trapped in a shadowy realm with nothing but an irritable maiden for company. Whatever the future held, he still had a rough road to travel before he reached that happy ending.

"Is this as bright as it gets?" He waved his good arm at the dark forest, the dimly glowing flowers scattered beneath feathery ferns.

"It is." The hint of a smile lurked in her voice. "This is the doublemoon—when both the palemoon and the bright ascend together into the sky. On the morrow, we'll be left with only one."

"I fervently hope it's the brighter one."

"Alas." Now she was outright laughing at him. "The brightmoon will not show itself until the palemoon has soared the sky thrice."

"So you spend your days stumbling about in the dark?" He certainly didn't welcome the idea.

"Of course not. My kind can summon light at will. And I believe our eyes have a greater ability to adjust to shades of brightness than your poor mortal vision."

They rode in silence for a time as Kent pondered her words. Around them, the Darkwood was unchanging: a carpet of velvety moss interspersed with fallen evergreen needles, the black columns of the trees rising in every direction, the occasional shaft of moonlight drifting down through an opening in the interlaced branches.

He could barely make out the shapes of fallen logs or the contours of the bushes ahead—and this was the brightest this realm became?

"Can you enchant my eyes, so that I might see better in the dim light?" he finally asked. He wouldn't admit how poor his vision was, for fear she'd take advantage and flee.

"Is that your heart's desire?" she asked, a teasing note in her voice.

"I'll pretend you didn't ask me that."

A soft chuckle, and then he felt her lean forward, her breath against his neck once more.

"It is possible, I suppose," she said. "Let me think upon it."

He nodded. Such a small enchantment should be within her powers—though he'd make absolutely sure she knew it was *not* the wish he claimed in return for her capture. If he'd learned anything from his fable-reading, it was that magical creatures could twist the terms of any bargain, and that mortals had best take care.

CHAPTER 4

As they rode, Fanya pondered the human's request. She knew the rune to call light, of course—*calya*—and several others that created a small glamour, such as adding extra sparkle to gems or a sheen to her court gowns. Perhaps a combination of the two would work.

"I will attempt to enchant your vision," she told Prince Kentry the next time they halted for a rest.

"Just to be clear," he said, moving stiffly to perch on a nearby fallen log, "this is *not* my heart's desire."

"Understood." She nodded gravely, pretending she actually had the power to perform such a life-changing magic as reading his heart and making that wish come true.

She started by quickly refreshing the healing rune on his arm, frowning at the reddened flesh surrounding the arrow hole. It was not mending at all, and she worried that he might develop wound-fever. She added a murmured rune of pain-ease over the injury, and he drew in a deep, relieved breath. Clearly, he'd been concealing the extent of his discomfort.

Once she was finished with his arm, she came to stand before him. He watched her calmly.

"Close your eyes," she said.

He did, and she rested her fingertips gently over his eyebrows, trying to ignore how her pulse jumped. Truly, this wasn't a difficult thing she was about to attempt. Why her breath should be trembling, she could not say.

"*Calyagalad*," she said, drawing upon her wellspring and directing the power through her hands.

Blue light flared across her fingers, throwing his face into sharp relief, then fading. Slowly, she pulled her hands away.

"Open your eyes."

He did, blinking. A hint of astonishment crossed his face as he turned his head, looking at the trees, the flowers, and then her.

"Astounding." His gaze held hers. "Thank you, Fanya. I no longer feel as if I'm stumbling about in a dark room."

"Good. If, once we reach Nightshade, the light becomes too bright, tell me. I should be able to remove the enchantment." At least, she hoped so.

He nodded, and they mounted and recommenced their journey through the Erynvorn.

The palemoon had fled from the sky, and the brightmoon was dipping low when they finally reached a small clearing where they could make camp. As soon as Prince Kentry halted his horse, Fanya slipped lightly off and laid her hand against its warm back in gratitude for bearing her.

The prince dismounted more slowly, wincing in pain from the movement. A sluggish flow of blood had begun trickling from the arrow-hole in his arm, and she frowned in sympathy. Once she'd foraged for their dinner, she'd once again tend to the injury as best she could. It was her fault he was wounded, after all.

Though it was also his fault, for capturing her in the first place...

"This is where we'll spend the night?" He turned in a slow circle, then glanced up at the star-specked sky.

"Yes." She indicated the tumble of boulders on one side of the clearing. "We'll sleep beneath the shelter of the rocks. Now, rest. I'll fetch water."

"Here." He unslung an empty water skin from his belt and handed it to her.

Soft-footed, Fanya made her way to the stream that lay deeper in the Erynvorn. She filled his container, and her own, with the clear sweet water. On the way back, she gathered a pouchful of tart red berries and the long, moist shelf of a tree-growing mushroom.

Those, plus the supplies she carried in her pack, should feed them well enough. She didn't know if Kentry would have anything to contribute. He seemed rather ill-provisioned for a trip into the forest. Mortals were strange creatures.

Though not without their small charms.

He'd borne up stoically, though she knew his arm pained him with every movement. Despite that, he'd met her pointed words with jabs of own, which she couldn't help but admire. In the Moonflower Court, she was often chided for her sharp tongue.

Though, if she were a warrior instead of the youngest daughter of the Moonflower Lord and Lady, such bluntness would be appreciated, not frowned upon.

The fact that this mortal prince didn't feel any need to mince words with her made her like him all the better. Even if he thought she was an enchanted deer. He was clever, too. The suggestion she enchant his vision had been a good one, and she was pleased she'd been able to create a rune to suit.

When she returned to the clearing, she found that Kentry had made the rudiments of their camp, despite his injury.

"You were supposed to rest," she reminded him, glancing at the unsaddled horse that now browsed the clearing, the armfuls of long grasses he'd cut and laid at the foot of the stones to cushion their sleep.

"I did." He lifted his uninjured shoulder in a shrug. "For a short time, anyway."

She deposited the food she'd gathered on a flat stone and went to fetch the cheese and last bit of bread from her pack. The prince rummaged in his satchel and brought out dried fruit and a small piece of salted meat.

"I'm sorry I don't have more," he said. "I didn't expect… this." He looked at her, then the cedars towering above them.

"Do you have any bedding?" she asked, though she feared the answer was clear enough.

"Just my cloak. It won't get too cold, will it?"

"No—perhaps a bit cooler than it is now, once the brightmoon sets." She was reluctant to add her fear that he'd become feverish. Even with magical healing, wounds sometimes went bad.

But tomorrow they would reach Nightshade, and the healer there was certainly skilled enough to tend this stray human.

Then what?

Her mind shied from the question. Her current task was to bring Kentry safely out of the Erynvorn. Whatever happened after that was in the Oracle's hands.

"Come, sit by me and let me tend to that," she said, nodding to his arm.

He dabbed at the ooze of blood on his upper arm, then looked at his fingers, smeared faintly with red. "It doesn't hurt."

"Whether or not it does, it's never a good idea to bleed in the middle of the Erynvorn." She patted the grass covered ground beside her.

"The Erynvorn." He glanced at the trees surrounding their small clearing. "In my land, we call this forest the Darkwood."

"It is the same meaning," she said.

"I like your language better." He sent her a quick grin, then held out his arm. "Do your magic."

She poured a little water over the wound, wiping the liquid gently away with a torn-off strip of her undertunic and taking care not to touch the injury itself. Then she held her hand just above his arm and closed her eyes, reaching within herself for her wellspring of power.

As she'd not been healer-trained, she only knew those two runes; one to ease pain and the other to staunch blood and knit together small wounds. The hole in Kentry's arm could not be called small, of course, but her meager efforts would have to suffice until they reached the Nightshade Court.

She spoke both runes, infusing them with as much power as she could, conscious of his intent gaze as she worked. When she finished, she glanced into his face, glad to see that the lines of pain creasing his forehead had eased once more.

"Thank you," he said.

"Since I caused your injury, it's only fair that I tend it. But soon enough you'll be healed entirely, and free to return to your own land."

"With my wish granted," he reminded her.

Since she had no idea how to do such a thing, she made no reply. Instead, she turned to the flat stone and busied herself with portioning out their food.

They took their meal, though the prince was clearly distrustful of the mushroom, and only ate sparingly of the berries.

"I'm not trying to poison you," she said. "Eat. Your body needs fuel."

Slowly, he picked up a slice of mushroom and sniffed it. "It's unfamiliar."

"This whole realm is unfamiliar to you," she pointed out, a bit tartly. "That doesn't mean you must starve to death."

He shook his head, then took a bite of the mushroom and chewed it slowly. "I hope you have better food at your courts."

"I didn't think it wise to light a cooking fire. But I assure you, my people don't subsist on raw foods gleaned from the forest."

His eyebrows twitched, but he finished the piece of mushroom. She noticed he didn't reach for any more.

The last golden radiance faded as the brightmoon slipped away behind the trees, chasing the absent palemoon. A bird chirped sleepily from a nearby thicket, and the glowing blossoms of the *quille* furled themselves into shadow. Fanya tidied up the remains of their meal, then took her spidersilk blanket from her pack.

Normally she bound the two edges together with a simple rune, creating an envelope to sleep within—but it was large enough to spread over two, if they settled next to one another. She didn't welcome the thought of lying beside Kentry all night, but he was her responsibility, and she would let no harm come to him.

Speaking of which, she needed to set the wards about their camp, before the darkness brought anything unpleasant their way.

"If you need a moment," she said to the prince, "best take it now. I will be warding the clearing, and once the protections are in place, you cannot cross them."

"Why not?" He gave her a keen glance, curiosity glinting in his dark brown eyes. "Will the enchantment hurt me?"

"No. It will simply dispel, leaving us vulnerable."

"Can I watch you cast them?"

"I suppose there's no harm in it—but I doubt you'll be able to see anything."

He nodded, then rose to tend to his needs. In his absence, Fanya spread her silken blanket over the mounded grass he'd gathered for their simple bed. She did not like it, but there was no other option.

When the prince returned, he rinsed his hands and splashed water on his face, leaving a small amount in his waterskin. He glanced at the bed, then back to her.

"Where will I sleep?"

She shot him a look. "Do you think I mean to take all the comfort for myself and leave you on the hard ground?"

Color reddened his face and he glanced away. "I didn't want to presume. But if you're inviting me to share your bed—"

"I am not. We will simply sleep next to one another, for warmth." And so that, if he took a turn for the worse in the dark hours, she would sense it and be able to tend him.

"Ah." He nodded sagely. "For warmth."

Now it was her turn to blush.

"You're wounded," she said. "And even if you were not, I do not find you appealing in that manner."

Which, she had to privately admit, was an untruth. Though his features were not as sharp as those of her people, she found his full mouth and the soft planes of his cheeks appealing. The warmth in his eyes reminded her of the taste of dark honey, and for a fleeting moment she wondered how his hair would look, grown long and braided in the fashion of the warriors of Elfhame.

He raised a clenched fist to his heart. "You wound me! I am considered one of the most handsome men in Raine."

"I *have* wounded you, yes." She gave his injured arm a significant glance. "And as for what passes as comeliness among humans, I cannot say."

"You would be thought quite beautiful." There was no mockery in his voice. "By mortal standards, at least."

She ducked her head, letting her hair cover her blush with a silvery veil. By the moons, this human had a surprising ability to discomfit her.

Well, he would be gone soon enough, and then she wouldn't have to worry about how uncomfortable he made her. Strangely, she did not welcome the thought.

CHAPTER 5

Kent lay beside Fanya, staring up at the unfamiliar stars spangling the deep violet-black of the sky. He was tired, his body heavy with exhaustion, but his clamoring thoughts would not still enough for him to find sleep.

His moonlit-haired companion slept—or at least he thought she did. After their meal, she'd walked a circle about their campsite, humming beneath her breath and pausing at what he guessed had been each of the four directions. Although he'd watched her closely, he could detect no signs of magic, but he trusted her word that she'd set protective enchantments around them.

The magic she'd performed on his eyes, however, was much more tangible. The soft radiance of her realm bathed his vision, and though it wasn't like moving about in the sunlit world, he'd adjusted readily enough.

Her healing magic wasn't as effective, unfortunately, although when she'd murmured the strange, liquid syllables over the injury one last time before they took their rest, he'd sighed with relief. The waves of pain receded like the tide pulling away from the shore. The discomfort would be back, he knew, but hopefully not soon.

He didn't tell her that he felt hot and restless. Even if the wound was beginning to fester, there was nothing Fanya could do to aid him. Tomorrow they would reach the court she'd told him of. Nightshade.

It did not sound appealing. He imagined a dark and eerie place, filled with purple shadows and strange, pale beings who would not be pleased to see a human in their midst.

But they would heal him, and then Fanya would grant his heart's desire.

Although…he had to admit that the burning devotion for Maired he carried like a coal in his chest had cooled, ever since he'd chased the White Hart into this strange realm. But surely, once he returned to Raine, the force of his yearning would again pierce him with every breath he drew.

And, even better, Maired would love him back as passionately as he loved her. He pulled the knowledge over him, as comforting as the wood-smoke smell of his cloak laid atop them. Finally, he slept.

Fanya woke suddenly, her senses humming. Something had triggered her wards of protection.

Slowly, she reached for the bow set on the ground beside her. Once her fingers were wrapped about the grip, she sat in one smooth motion, pulling an arrow from her quiver and nocking it to the string.

Bow drawn, she scanned the shadows beneath the trees.

Nothing stirred. Her pulse beat through her, hollow and insistent.

Then, suddenly, a rush of air over her head. She sprang to her feet, calling out the rune for foxfire. The blue light illuminated the underside of batlike wings, the sinuous neck and baleful eye of a drake as it passed overhead.

"Prince," she said softly, nudging his sleeping her form with her foot. "Awaken."

In credit to his obvious warrior training, it took only a single heartbeat for him to roll from beneath his cloak and draw the sword he'd kept sheathed on his side of their makeshift bed.

"What is it?" His voice was heavy with sleep, and he blinked, squinting at the clearing. "Are we under attack?"

"Imminently—from above. My wards will deflect one strike, but after that, we'll be unprotected."

"Not entirely." He shot her a tight look. "Good thing you didn't shoot my sword arm. What's after us?"

"A drake. Luckily a small one, by the look—"

Her words were cut off by an angry shriek as the creature plunged down, wickedly sharp claws extended. The horse, tethered nearby, let out a shrill whinny of fear, and Fanya spared a sliver of hope that the drake would leave it alone.

She tilted her bow up, aiming for one of the drake's yellow eyes, and let her arrow fly. It struck the creature near the mouth, which seemed to enrage it. Her wards of protection flared blue, and then were gone.

"Take cover beside the rock." Kentry gestured. "You shoot at the beast while I keep it distracted."

"Beware the claws," she said, stepping back. "They're poisonous."

"Wonderful. Here it comes."

He moved away from their sleeping area, giving himself room to maneuver, and Fanya set another arrow to her bow.

"Strike the underbelly," she called. "It's not as heavily scaled there."

At least, not according to the few accounts of how to fight drakes she'd found in the Moonflower scrolls while researching creatures of the Erynvorn. The best hope for a fatal blow, however, was an eye shot. The stories she'd read had not mentioned how difficult that would be. The drake's head was set at the end of a long, scaly neck, which whipped about constantly.

The creature descended and Kentry ducked, swiping at its belly. His sword flashed blue in the light of her foxfire. The blade grated across the drake's scales, doing no noticeable damage, and the prince was barely able to avoid a vicious rake of the creature's claws. Fanya kept her arrow trained on its head, but it moved too quickly for her to be sure of hitting her mark.

With effort, she kept her breathing controlled, her hands steady. There wouldn't be many chances to make her shot, and when one came, she must be prepared. No matter that her blood raced with fear, that the looming jaws of death gaped wide above their heads.

As the drake made another pass, Kentry stabbed up at its belly with the tip of his sword. The creature screeched as the blade penetrated. Thick, dark blood dripped from the injury and fell, sizzling, upon the ground. The prince wrenched his blade free and dodged away as the drake darted its head down with a vicious snap of teeth.

So far, Kentry had managed to stay away from the creature's attacks, but Fanya saw how clumsy his movements were growing. A sheen of sweat covered his face, and his blade wavered as he held it at the ready.

With another screech, the drake backwinged into the air, keeping its baleful yellow gaze on Kentry. It was poised for another diving attack—but that momentary pause in the air was all Fanya needed. She sighted along her arrow, then let it fly.

It struck the creature directly in the eye. Shrieking, the drake turned toward the rock where she sheltered, and dove directly at her.

"Fanya!" the prince cried, horror in his voice.

She dropped into a roll, desperately trying to avoid the drake's poisonous claws. A touch along her back, feather-light. He jerkin parted, her skin stung. The creature let out a bellow and made an ungainly landing, then lurched around to face her once more.

Shouting, Kentry threw himself forward and plunged his sword into the drake's other eye.

It froze, swayed, and then, with a gurgle, collapsed upon the trampled grasses.

They stared at the fallen drake a moment, and Fanya felt a trembling wave sweep from her legs up through her whole body. Grimacing, Kentry wrenched his sword out of the creature's eye, then wiped the blade clean and sheathed it. He plucked the arrow from its other eye, and brought it to Fanya.

"Did it touch you?" he asked.

Still kneeling, she reached to take the arrow, then winced at the flare of fire between her shoulders.

"I...think it did." Slowly, she turned so that he might view her back.

A hiss as he sucked air through his teeth. Gently, he folded her jerkin away from her skin. "It scratched you—lightly, but enough to draw blood. Is the poison…" He faltered, voice catching. "Does it act quickly, or do you have time?"

"Don't worry—I won't drop dead at your feet." At least, she didn't think so. "But we must head for Nightshade immediately."

"I don't think I'd fancy sleeping next to a dead drake, in any case," he said, then laid his cool fingers upon her back. "Do you have something I could clean and bandage this with?"

"I'll tear strips from the blanket." She went to their makeshift bed and sank down upon the piled grasses.

With the help of the small dagger she kept belted at her waist, she set about ruining her silk blanket. While she was at it, she tore several extra pieces to use as new dressings for his arm.

"Won't you need that?" he asked, watching as she shredded the cloth.

She glanced up at him, noting the pallor of his face, the shadows beneath his eyes.

"Either we'll take our next rest in beds at the Nightshade Court, or we'll have no need of blankets ever again."

He gave her a grim nod. "At least the creature didn't attack my horse. As soon as you're tended to, I'll saddle up and we'll go. Can you bring your light a bit closer?"

Through he tried to be gentle as he dabbed at her back with a water-dampened piece of silk, she winced whenever he touched the scratch.

"I presume you can cast your healing magic upon yourself," he said. "Will it help slow the poison's effect?"

"I don't know. But I'll try."

She murmured the runes, dismayed to find her wellspring sluggish and partially depleted. It seemed that the drake's inimical touch affected the source of her power, as well as her flesh and blood—though the stories had made no mention of that effect.

"Let me tend to you, as well," she said, neglecting to add that her powers were fading.

She would do what she could for both of them, then pray to the brightmoon that they reached Nightshade alive.

CHAPTER 6

KENT BLINKED, his vision blurry. Something lay ahead, but he didn't know whether it was a fever mirage brought on by the relentless hours of their journey, or the Nightshade Court at last. Certainly the pale, gracefully-arched palace shining faintly under the sickle of the small moon didn't match his dire imaginings.

Perhaps it was an illusion after all.

After they'd left the clearing where they'd defeated the drake, he and Fanya had spent an eternity riding through the huge, dark forest. They'd taken turns supporting one another through the long hours, coaxing each other to drink, one holding the other upright when either of them veered into unconsciousness—which happened more often the longer they traveled.

They'd tried placing Fanya in front of him as they rode—but any time his clothing brushed against the thin, angry line across her back, she winced. So she rode behind him, her arms about his waist, her head resting against his shoulders as they both fought to remain awake.

Eventually, the palemoon had risen, sending a soft lavender light through the trees. Some endless time after that, they'd passed from riding between the huge columns of the evergreens to smaller stands of white-barked saplings that shivered with every breeze. Following Fanya's murmured instructions, he'd guided Nimble through silvery swaths of meadow grass and past a quiet lake rimmed with phosphorescence.

And now, he hardly dared hope, they'd finally arrived at their destination.

"Fanya." He reached behind him and gently touched her leg. "Is that the Nightshade Court?"

She murmured and stirred, and he felt her lift her head from his shoulder.

"Yes." Her breath whispered past his ear. "Make for the main gates."

A smooth dirt road curved to intersect their course, leading to the wide, pillared opening framing the palace. As they passed through, Kent noted filigreed gates, folded back like wings against the graceful outer walls.

A stretch of garden, planted with beds of pale flowers and trailing vines, lay between the gates and the long building ahead. Slender turrets rose at either end of the palace, and lights glimmered from multiple arched openings that must be windows.

Lights danced about him and Fanya, too, as they rode forward; small balls of radiance that looped over their heads and then darted back toward the palace.

"Glimglows," Fanya said. "They will alert the Nightshade Lord and Lady of our arrival."

He might have been apprehensive at the thought of

meeting the monarchs, but sheer exhaustion, coupled with the pounding fever in his head, blunted all else.

Perhaps he drifted into unconsciousness, for it seemed that between one eyeblink and the next they arrived at the front door of the palace. Three wide, flat steps mounted to an arched doorway surrounded by carved vines and leaves. Instead of torches, the doorway was flanked by crystal bowls holding the strange blue lights he'd seen Fanya conjure.

A moment later, they were surrounded by four stern elvish warriors. Despite their long, intricately braided hair, and the fact that two of them were women, they had the air of hardened fighters. Kent drew his horse to a halt, careful to keep his hand well away from his sword.

"Who are you?" the lead warrior demanded, staring intently at Kent. "And what have you done to Lady Fanyaleth?"

"Peace, Pilinor," Fanya said. "He saved my life."

"But he is a mortal." The warrior gave her a distrustful look.

"Even so," she said.

"What call have you to bring such a one—"

"The lady is wounded and in need of healing," Kent broke in, little caring for the formalities. "We both are. Such discussions can wait until later."

The warrior's brows rose, but the brusqueness of Kent's words didn't seem to anger him.

"Then we shall escort you to the healer. Naica, Hatal, assist Lady Fanyaleth. Ileth and I will keep watch on this one." He turned his pointed gaze back to Kent.

Gently, the assigned warriors helped Fanya dismount.

Kent followed, though he received only suspicious looks instead of careful assistance as he slid from his horse.

"Will you tend to Nimble?" he asked, patting his horse's withers. "He's carried us faithfully." He kept himself from asking if they even knew what such things as horses were. After all, Fanya had seemed comfortable with his mount.

"A servant will take your horse to the stables," the warrior, Pilinor, said. "Now, come."

He led the way up the steps, Kent and his watchful guard behind, and then Fanya with her escort. As they passed through the arched doorway into a long corridor, the air turned pleasantly warm. More of the blue lights glowed at intervals, their soft radiance reflected by the polished marble walls and floor.

For a court named Nightshade, the surroundings were far more airy and graceful than Kent had imagined. Although, on closer inspection, the carvings of foliage about the doors did, indeed, depict that poisonous plant.

Pilinor turned left down a smaller hallway, then right at another, which soon opened into an atrium. A quiet fountain plashed in the center of the room, and a half-dozen beds were arranged along the far wall.

A silver-haired elf woman sat before a table, but quickly rose as they entered. Unlike Fanya and the warriors, she wore a gown, made of rich blue cloth. Her gaze fell upon Kent for a moment, then went to Fanya.

"Lady Fanyaleth," she exclaimed in concern, hurrying to meet them. "Your wellspring is dangerously low. And what poison is that I sense within you?"

"Drake," Fanya said, weaving slightly on her feet.

"Help her to sit," the healer said, gesturing to the nearest bed.

"My companion is wounded, as well," Fanya said, nodding at Kent.

"It can wait," he said, his own dismay ticking up at the healer's worried expression. "See to the lady."

Fanya's escorts assisted her to the bed. Kent followed, trailed by his own watchful guard, while Pilinor took up a post near the fountain, one hand resting on his sword.

"Can you heal her, Mistress Silweth?" the warrior asked.

"I believe so."

"And what of the mortal?"

The healer glanced at Kent. "A simple enough injury." She waved at the next bed over. "There is no need to hover, human. Rest, while I tend to Lady Fanyaleth. I sense a great weariness within you."

Reluctantly, Kent moved to the bed and slowly sat. The coverlet was woven of a soft gray material and the mattress gave slightly beneath his weight. With a narrow-eyed look, the warrior guarding him moved to stand at the end of the bed.

Kent didn't care. He harbored no ill-will toward the inhabitants of Nightshade. All his concern was for Fanya, whose pale skin seemed even paler, the silver luster of her hair faded as she gingerly lay down upon her side, facing the bed where he sat. She smiled faintly at him—more a grimace than anything—and Kent leaned forward, ignoring the throbbing pain in his arm. *Be strong*, he willed at her as their gazes met.

Her smile fell and she winced as the healer examined her back. From where he sat, Kent had a clear view of Mistress Silweth's expression, which didn't bode well.

"You *can* heal her, can't you?" he demanded.

"Hush," Pilinor said from his post by the fountain.

The healer didn't respond, but bent to her work. Her long fingers left glowing sigils in the air as she chanted. To Kent's relief, the pain in Fanya's eyes eased.

"You should rest," Fanya said to him.

"No." Despite the heavy exhaustion blurring his senses, he refused to close his eyes until he knew that, when he opened them again, she would still be there.

"At least lie down," she said.

"Sh. Don't worry about me."

She nodded, once, then drew in a halting breath as the healer touched her back again.

"It will take several turns for me to drive all the poison out," Mistress Silweth said. "But you will recover. That, I promise. When did you last eat?"

Fanya blinked. "I…not since last moonset."

Mistress Silweth frowned and sent one of Fanya's escort off immediately to bring food. Then she turned to Kent and peeled away the makeshift bandages around his arm. When she spoke the healing words, a great rush of ease went through him, and the bone-deep agony within him quieted.

"Thank you," he said.

"You are not fully mended," Mistress Silweth said. "You must take care with your arm for some time yet."

"Can I stay here?" He looked at Fanya, who was still watching him. Truly, he didn't know where else he might go. She was his only friend in this strange world.

"The Nightshade rulers will wish to speak with him," Pilinor said.

"Might it wait?" Fanya asked softly. "I would stand at his side."

The warrior looked displeased, but it seemed her request carried enough weight to silence his protests.

Time passed in a blur. Kent slept, ate, slept again, though most of his attention was focused on Fanya. The healer performed enchantments upon her twice more, and with each healing session she seemed improved.

In the quietest hours of the night, however, the drake's poison roused for a final attempt.

The room was dim, the fountain still, when Fanya's whimpers of pain woke Kent.

"Fanya?" He sat, blessing the enchantment upon his eyes that enabled him to see in the faint light.

She tossed upon her bed, her hair stuck damply to her face with perspiration. Quickly, he rose and dipped a pitcher of water from the fountain's basin, as the elves had done. He coaxed her to drink, then dampened a cloth and gently sponged her forehead.

When the worst of her fever passed, he made to rise, but she gripped his hand fiercely.

"Stay," she whispered.

"I will. Give me a moment."

He loosened her grasp and went to push his bed up beside hers. His arm twinged at the motion, but he paid it no heed. When he lay back down, she reached for him again, curling her hands about his. He bowed his head, their foreheads touching, and took a deep breath.

For the first time in months, Kent passed the rest of the night in a deep and dreamless slumber.

In the morning, the healer's brows rose, but she said nothing about the new proximity of their beds. She frowned when Kent told her of Fanya's fever in the night, but reassured him that the healing was well underway—for both of them.

CHAPTER 7

"Lady Fanyaleth!"

The summons woke Fanya, and she blinked in momentary confusion, trying to orient herself. The soft splash of the fountain in the healer's enclave of the Nightshade Court, the soft radiance of foxfire—and the warmth of Kentry's hand in hers, their fingers entwined, his bed pushed beside hers.

"What is it?" She slid her hand from his grasp and sat.

He woke, too, and looked up at her, his brown eyes confused. The vulnerability in their depths made something within her twist with yearning.

"Yes?" She glanced at the doorway where the warrior, Pilinor, stood.

"An Oracle has come," he said. "They request an audience."

Of course. She looked at the mortal by her side. Her prophecy had sent her into the Erynvorn, where she'd found Prince Kentry. Now, his time in Elfhame was drawing to a close. She refused to acknowledge how her heart ached at the thought.

"Prince," she said softly, bending over him. "I have a confession to make." Now that the Oracle was at hand, there was no more use in pretending. "I am not actually the White Hart."

His brows drew together briefly, and then he smiled at her. "I know. Once we arrived at the court, I guessed as much."

Before she could say anything more, a figure stepped into the room, garbed head to toe in white. The veil covering their head made it impossible to tell their gender, and their low, mellifluous voice gave no further clues.

"Lady Fanyaleth of the Moonflower Court," the Oracle said, halting a few paces from her bedside, "I am here to complete the circle of your prophecy."

Fanya nodded, and swung her legs over the edge of the bed. She'd prefer to meet her fate standing. To her surprise, Kentry also rose and came to stand at her side.

"I'm ready," she said.

For whatever reason, the Oracles had sent her into the forest so that she might find this mortal prince and bring him safely to Nightshade. Now that he was healed, they would return him to the mortal world so that he might fulfill whatever destiny awaited him.

And for herself?

She supposed she'd return, a dutiful daughter of Moonflower, and resign herself to an advantageous political marriage with one of the other courts. The thought pulled upon her heart, and she refused to consider it too closely.

"Are you?" The Oracle sounded lightly amused. "And what of you, Prince Kentry of Raine? Are you ready to achieve your heart's desire?"

Fanya was conscious of the prince's gaze upon her, but she didn't—couldn't—return it. Something inside her was cracking in two, and she dared not name the sorrow rending her.

"I believe I am," Kentry said.

The Oracle bowed their veiled head. "Am I to send you back to the mortal world, then?"

The prince cleared his throat. "Actually, I have a question."

Fanya sent him a startled glance, and he slanted her a quick smile in return.

"What is your question?" the Oracle asked.

"If you sent me back to the mortal world," he said, "would I ever be able to return here?"

"No. The gate can only be opened once more."

Kentry blew out his breath, then caught Fanya's hand. His fingers were warm against hers, his clasp firm.

"Fanya," he said, turning to her, "I thought I knew what my heart's desire was…until I met you."

"What did you wish?" she asked, an unaccountable tightness in her chest.

His lips twisted into a crooked smile. "I wished that a certain lady would love me. And yet, the longer I was away, the less I thought of her. My feelings for her were a grassfire —hot and bright, and, ultimately, short-lived."

"What, then, is your heart's desire?" the Oracle asked him.

"I…" Kentry held Fanya's gaze. "If my love for that lady was a fire, now burnt away, I believe that you have planted a seed in my heart. I would very much like to see the tall tree it will grow into, if given a chance. Would you be willing to take me to your court, lady? To see what we might achieve, together?"

The sorrow ripping through Fanya mended in a wave of hope. "You would stay here? What of your mortal life?"

He shook his head. "I might not know the entirety of my heart's desire—yet. But I believe I will find it here, in your world."

Fanya closed her eyes. Opened them, and glanced at the white-veiled Oracle.

"It is your choice," the Oracle said. "Your birthright sent you into the Erynvorn for a reason."

That reason stood before her, entreaty in his mortal eyes. A memory of all they had endured together flashed through her. Prince Kentry of Raine—the courageous, irritating, handsome mortal man who wished to remain in Elfhame. With her.

"If you will take such a leap," she said to him, "then I can do no less. Prince Kentry of Raine, will you stay with me, in this realm?"

His smile blazed and she thought she'd never tire of the look in his eyes—warmth, admiration, companionship, and the seed of a deep love, waiting to open.

"Lady Fanyaleth, I desire nothing more."

"You are certain?" the Oracle asked.

Kentry nodded. "My future is here, at the side of this moon-haired maiden. Whatever may come."

"Then so be it," the Oracle said. "May your lives be long and filled with joy." They bowed their veiled head and began a soft chant of blessing.

As the Oracle's favor drifted over them, Fanya gripped Kent's hand.

"Do you fear you'll regret this choice?" she asked softly, staring into his eyes.

He met her gaze steadily, his clasp firm. "Never. This is my heart's desire."

His heart's desire. And hers. Twined together by fate.

It was all the answer she needed.

~*~

THE GIFT OF LOVE

Twang! The unmistakable sound of a gittern string breaking echoed through the Bardic Collegium's wood-paneled rehearsal room, accompanied by youthful laughter.

Bard Shandara Tem kept her smile on her face, despite her exasperation, and glanced to her left, at the soprano section of the Bardic Trainee's Ensemble.

"Would you like assistance tuning, Jaya?" she asked the red-faced girl sitting up front.

"I know how to tune up," the girl said. "Honestly. I think the string was just weak. But, if you could help me put on a new one?"

Shandara nodded and took the gittern. Like most Bards, she had a solid acquaintance with most instruments, though her main proficiency was on the harp.

Quickly, she re-strung the top course of Jaya's gittern and handed it back to the girl. Already, the babble in the room was growing louder. Too long an interruption, and the two dozen members of the ensemble would veer into cheerful chaos. Many of them were of an age where teasing denoted signs of affection, and with the Vernal Equinox approaching, the intensity of their young emotions was almost overwhelming.

"Trainees!" Shandara pitched her voice to cut through the noise. "Focus, please. We only have a week before the performance."

She hadn't chosen to lead the ensemble's rehearsals, but the Bard who directed the Trainees had been called away on a family emergency.

"You're best suited to take over," her mentor, Master Bard Tangeli, had said with a brief, sympathetic smile. "The Trainees have been working hard for their performance at the Spring Fair this month. We can't disappoint them."

Or their families, of course. Parents of the Trainees often made a special effort to attend the Fairs and cheer their offspring on. Seeing their students perform was a high point, and it was up to Shandara to make sure the ensemble was at their best.

Given the general disorganization in the rehearsal room, however, Shandara wasn't sure her charges were equally dedicated to their upcoming performance. The amount of foolery and shenanigans she'd witnessed in the past two weeks was impressive, even for Trainees with an overabundance of romantic longings.

In addition to suspiciously regular incidents of instruments going awry, the tried-and-true practice of switching sections to fool the new director (it hadn't taken Shandara long to sort them all back out again), and sheet music getting ridiculously shuffled, the sopranos had managed to fall an entire measure behind during the last rehearsal, and the piece had dissolved into giggles.

The main instigator seemed to be a boy named Edwold.

The moment Jaya's string broke, he'd bent over with laughter. With an inward sigh, Shandara turned to him. "Edwold, I think we should go over your solo section."

In her limited experience, she'd found that nothing was better guaranteed to settle young spirits down than putting them to work. Edwold was one of the two soloists chosen for the performance. His high, clear voice was perfectly suited to the descant lines in the closing ballad of the performance.

The grin fell from his face.

"I don't feel well, Bard Shandara," he said, a slight shake in his voice. "Can't we do it next rehearsal?"

She studied him. He'd gone pale, and though she knew he was a consummate actor, it seemed as though he was telling the truth.

"Very well," she said. "I'll hear you tomorrow. Now, everyone, let's try 'The Sparrows Aloft.' Jaya, the first chord, if you will."

The girl strummed a tuneful chord, the Trainees settled, and soon the strains of the celebratory piece filled the air. Shandara kept a close watch on Edwold, but he remained perfectly well behaved for the rest of the rehearsal.

She had no doubt that on the morrow, however, he'd be back to his mischievous ways.

"I don't know what I'm going to do about Edwold," Shandara said, taking a thoughtful sip of tea.

She and her friends, Healer Tarek and Trainee Lyssa, had gathered in her rooms for dinner and were companionably seated around her small, round table. A cozy fire crackled in the hearth, taking the cold edge off the air as they finished up their meal.

"He's just a boy," Tarek said, mopping up the last bit of sauce on his plate with a hunk of bread. "Probably sweet on that girl Jaya, and worried about embarrassing himself at the Spring Fair. He'll settle down."

"I hope that's the case. But I can't help feeling it's something more."

Lyssa shot her a glance, her sweet face concerned. "My Empathy is getting stronger as my training progresses. If you'd like, I could come listen to the rehearsal tomorrow—and pay special attention to Edwold."

"Would you? I'd appreciate any insight you might have." Shandara reached over and squeezed her young friend's arm.

Lyssa was a Mind Healer, a rare Gift. If anyone could ferret out what was at the heart of Edwold's troublemaking, it would be her.

"Speaking of the Spring Fair, is there anyone you're planning on attending with, Lyssa?" Tarek gave her a wink.

The girl made a face. "All the boys my age are silly. A group of us girls are planning to wander about together."

"Wise," Tarek said. "I don't blame you in the least. I was impossible at that age."

"Only a handful of years ago, as I recall," Shandara said, teasing him.

Tarek put a hand to his chest. "Me? Never. You're thinking of my friend Ro. Who, as I'll remind you, is now happily wed."

Lyssa cleared her throat and gave Tarek a significant look. "Married. And he's your age."

"He finished at Collegium before I did," Tarek said. "Besides, the expectations are different for lordlings."

Shandara noted the tips of his ears had reddened. She, too, was a little uncomfortable with Lyssa's not-so-subtle urgings toward matrimony. While Shandara was very fond of Tarek, they were both young yet—and he was still finding his footing as newly minted Healer. For now, she was content with their relationship. If, in the future, they were ready for more, well, they would face that decision together.

"After the Trainee Ensemble performs, I'll be free to wander the Fair with you," Shandara said, glancing at Lyssa, and then Tarek.

"I wouldn't want to interrupt the cooing of you two lovebirds." Lyssa gave them a smug look. "Besides, Tarek, you're a lordling, too."

"I'm a Healer first," he said, his voice clear with conviction.

Shandara sent him a warm smile. He'd had his own difficult journey, and she was glad to have been able to help along the way. Lyssa, too, had struggled with her Gift.

"Come with us after the concert," Shandara said, turning to the girl. "Spring Fair is about celebrating all the connections between people, don't forget. Friends and family count just as much as romantic interests."

Tarek gestured with his piece of bread. "Absolutely. And speaking of family, you can use us as an excuse to escape yours, any time."

"Thank you." Lyssa's tone turned serious. "You two know you're my *real* family here in Haven."

Shandara leaned over and squeezed the girl's shoulders. "We know."

"She's just angling for us to buy her a half-dozen pocket pies at the Fair," Tarek said, his grin showing he didn't mean it.

"Well of course." Lyssa blinked innocently at him. "Isn't that what families are for?"

The next afternoon, as promised, Lyssa arrived at the rehearsal room as the Trainee's Ensemble was gathering. She took a seat in the far corner and opened a book. A few of the young musicians glanced at her, but since she was clearly there with Shandara's permission, her presence was noted, then dismissed.

Wondering what the day's mischief might be, Shandara called the group to order.

"Let's start with the 'Ode to a Companion,'" she said. "Are you ready for your solo, Edwold?" Might as well begin with putting the lad in the spotlight, and see what happened.

"Yes, Bard Shandara," Edwold said, jumping up.

He took his place at the front, a light in his eyes that boded trouble. Shandara caught Lyssa's gaze. The girl glanced at Edwold, then back, her brow furrowed. Clearly something was afoot. Ah well, the only way to uncover it was to forge ahead.

"Jaya, the chord please," Shandara said.

The girl complied, and Shandara was glad to see that at least the instrument was behaving today. Even if there was a spate of muffled giggling from some of the boys.

She counted off, and the ensemble began. The song was a lovely composition about the bond between a Herald and her Companion—perfect as a finale for their Spring Fair performance. The full choral parts softened, and Shandara gestured to Edwold.

He opened his mouth for the first bars of his solo.

Croak. The unmistakable sound of a bullfrog sounded from somewhere about his person. Probably the pocket his hand was tucked firmly in. Shandara narrowed her eyes.

A half-dozen answering ribbits and croaks sounded from the back of the soprano section. The music dissolved, the melody lost under shrieks of laughter.

"Edwold." Shandara kept her tone stern, though she had to admit it was an amusing prank. Amusing—if they didn't have a performance looming in two days. And if it wasn't abundantly clear that Edwold was trying desperately to keep from performing his solo. "Please show me what's in your pocket."

The boy pulled out his hand. He held a fat brown frog with a green head, its long legs dangling down on either side of his palm.

It croaked again, blinking at the sudden light. For such a small creature, it produced an astonishingly loud sound. Again came answering noises from some of the other boys. The Trainees started to giggle again. Shandara waved her hand for silence, keeping her gaze fixed on Edwold.

"I'm sorry," he said, with false contritement. "I was out in the meadow before lunch with my friends. The frogs must have crawled into our pockets somehow."

"Somehow," Shandara said dryly. "Perhaps you and your co-conspirators can take them back to their preferred habitat. Now."

With a broad grin, Edwold nodded. "If you say so, Bard Shandara."

He jerked his head, and three other boys rose from the back of the ensemble. Their trousers were all muddy at the knees—no doubt from their frog-catching efforts.

"Ribbit," one of the boy's pockets said.

"Go." Shandara waved at the door. "When you return, we'll run the Ode again."

"Of course, Bard Shandara." Edwold gave her a jaunty wave and led his crew out of the room.

"Come back right away!" she called after their retreating backs. She had the sour suspicion they'd dawdle until rehearsal was over.

Drat. She shouldn't have said they'd practice the Ode.

From the back of the room, Lyssa gave her an eloquent look, eyebrows raised. Clearly, the girl had sensed something. Shandara could hardly wait to find out what it might be.

But first, they had the remainder of a rehearsal to get through.

"Trainees, while we wait for Edwold, let's run 'The Sparrow Aloft.'" Shandara raised her hands.

With the worst miscreants gone, the ensemble quickly settled. Soon, the sweet strains of voices interwoven with gittern and flute filled the room. They were a talented bunch. When they focused.

As she'd suspected, Edwold and his friends timed their return to coincide with the end of rehearsal.

"I'm sorry," he said, sounding completely unrepentant. "The frogs got away outside the Common Room, and we had to chase them down."

"Hm." Shandara stared at him a moment, then looked to Lyssa. Should she ask that the boy speak with her?

Lips compressed, Lyssa gave a slight nod. Clearly she'd sensed something. Edwold's behavior was more than just boyish pranks. Whatever was amiss, it was high time they uncover the problem.

"I expect dress rehearsal tomorrow to go smoothly," Shandara said. "It's our last scheduled practice. And I'm sure the rest of the Trainees would be unhappy to give up their free morning at the Fair because I had to call an emergency rehearsal the day of the performance. Do you understand?"

Edwold gulped, the smile falling from his face.

"Yes, Bard Shandara," he said meekly, dropping his gaze—but not before Shandara glimpsed something that looked like panic in his eyes.

"Good. Please see me in my rooms in fifteen minutes." She turned to the rest of the ensemble. "Don't forget the work we put in today with dynamics, everyone. And tenors, please go over your parts, especially the exposed sections. I'll see you all tomorrow."

She turned back to Edwold, but he was already gone, slipping out with his friends ahead of the rest of the students.

The last of the Trainees filtered from the room. Lyssa tucked her book under her arm and came to stand beside Shandara. The petite blonde's head barely came up to her shoulder, and Shandara blinked at the reminder of the girl's youth. Lyssa carried a maturity beyond her years—due in large part to the burden of her family's expectations, as well as her Gift.

"We should talk in your rooms before you meet with Edwold," Lyssa said.

"Certainly."

Shandara led the way through the halls of the Bardic Collegium, and tried not to worry. Whatever was wrong with Edwold, they had a mere two days to set things to rights.

∽

"You're right," Lyssa said, settling cross-legged in one of Shandara's upholstered armchairs and propping her chin in her hands. "My Empathy was definitely prickling during rehearsal. Edwold is distressed at the thought of performing his solo. That's why he's been doing everything he can to avoid singing it."

"Distressed? In what way?" Shandara paced before the window, unable to settle. "Can you tell, specifically, what the problem is? Stage fright?"

Lyssa shook her head. "I didn't get a sense of fear. More like an immense sorrow, and guilt. I think he *wants* to perform—he's proud of being chosen for a solo—but an even bigger part of him is swamped with fear at the thought."

Shandara let out a deep breath. Failure to prepare the Trainee's Ensemble for the Spring Fair performance would reflect badly on the entire Bardic Collegium—which meant she had to get to the bottom of Edwold's troubles as soon as possible.

"Is there anything else you can tell me?" Perhaps the boy had lied somehow in order to gain the solo—but that didn't make sense.

The students were hand-selected for the honor, and Shandara had heard Edwold sing before. He was talented, with a clear, sweet voice that hadn't yet deepened—a good choice to sing the part.

Perhaps that was it. "Do you think his voice is changing, and he's afraid to admit it?"

Lyssa firmed her lips in thought, then slowly shook her head. "I don't think so. His reaction felt…older, somehow. Not recent."

"Well, thank you." Shandara gave her friend a weary smile. "You've helped give me a direction to go, anyway."

"Of course." Lyssa jumped up. "Good luck talking to him!"

"Stay for a cup of tea?" Shandara went over to set the kettle beside her small hearth.

"No—Edwold will be here soon, and it's better if you talk with him privately, I think."

"You're right." Much as Shandara would have liked Lyssa's support, they didn't need to outnumber the boy.

Shandara gave the girl a hug as she left, then went to fix herself a cup of tea. And one for Edwold, too. As she was pouring hot water over the minty leaves, a soft knock came at her door.

"Come in," she called, setting down the kettle.

Edwold peeked around the oaken planks, anxiety clear in his expression. "You wanted to meet with me?"

"Yes." She gestured for him to come in and take a seat. "Tea?"

"All right." He took the cup she offered, then perched awkwardly on the edge of the same armchair Lyssa had inhabited. "I haven't done anything wrong."

"I didn't say you have," Shandara said mildly. "Although the frogs were a bit much, I think. And I'd prefer the instruments to stay in tune."

Edwold swallowed and glanced down at his tea, but said nothing in his own defense.

"You're a talented singer," Shandara continued, trying to feel her way forward. "I think Bard Alvee made a good choice, picking you for a solo, and I look forward to hearing you actually sing it. Are you ready for the dress rehearsal?"

At that, Edwold looked up, and she saw that same flash of panic cross his face.

"I..." His voice choked, then fell to a whisper. "I want to sing the solo. But I can't."

"Why not?" She kept her voice soft. Her Empathy was humming sympathetically with the force of his distress.

He shook his head, his expression miserable. "I just can't."

"Please, tell me why." She leaned forward, trying to project reassurance. It wasn't the first time she'd helped a young Trainee face what seemed an insurmountable problem. "Maybe I can help."

Edwold closed his eyes for a moment. When he opened them again, they were filled with the shine of sorrow. With a ragged breath, he set his cup aside, then clasped his hands tightly in his lap.

"My..." He glanced at the floor, then back at her. "My family will be at the Spring Fair. They're coming to Haven from our village on the coast. And I can't sing in front of them. I thought I could, but..." He blinked furiously to keep the tears back.

Had Master Tangeli been aware that beneath Edwold's cocky exterior, the boy was struggling? It would explain why the Master Bard had appointed her to take over the ensemble.

She studied Edwold, trying to get to the heart of the matter. "Why can't you sing for them?"

"It...wouldn't be right!" he blurted out, his voice catching. "My brother was supposed to be the Bard—not me. He was going to come to the Collegium, and be amazing, and make everyone proud. I stole his place. He should be here, and instead, I am—"

He broke off with a choked sob, and scrubbed his forearm

across his face. The misery rolling off him made her heart catch with mirrored sorrow.

"How old are you, Edwold?"

"Twelve." He cleared his throat. "I mean, next month."

"And what happened to your brother?"

He sniffed and looked away, out the window toward the view of the Companion's field. Shandara didn't press him. She leaned back and took a sip of tea, letting the silence lie easy in the room.

Several minutes passed, and Edwold seemed lost in his unhappy thoughts.

"When I first came to the Collegium," Shandara finally said, "everyone had such high expectations of me. Instead, I felt like I was moving backward. All my yearmates got their Scarlets, and I was still waiting for my Gift. For quite a while, I believed I was here by mistake."

"But I am!" Edwold turned to face her. "It was supposed to be Kendry."

"There's no rule that says siblings can't attend the Collegium together," Shandara said gently. "I've heard you sing, and you're very good. I'm certain you have the other talents necessary to become a Bard, as well. We don't admit people who don't belong here."

"Kendry was better," Edwold said. "And now, because of me, he's—he's dead."

Shandara blinked. Not what she'd expected the boy to say. No wonder Edwold was filled with guilt and sorrow.

"What happened?" she asked gently.

"Two years ago, the spring before Kendry was going to come to the Collegium, we were playing by the sea—we live near Kelmskeep—and the cliffside fell." He gulped, then continued. "We were down at the beach, and Ken noticed it first. I was closer to the cliff, and wasn't paying attention. He yelled at me to run, but I didn't hear. So he…he ran in and pushed me out of the way of the rock fall. And it crushed him."

Tears were rolling down the boy's face, and Shandara couldn't keep her own eyes dry.

"Oh, Edwold. May I give you a hug?" She opened her arms.

He nodded and scooted closer, letting her squeeze his shoulders. "Kendry was the best singer I've ever heard. My parents and sister are coming to the Spring Fair for the first time, and when they see me, when they hear me sing, they'll remember that it's supposed to be my brother. That he died because of me. They'll hate me for it!"

The boy's grief was tangible, and Shandara had to draw several breaths before she found her own balance. Surely everyone had told the boy it wasn't his fault, and that his family didn't hate him, but emotions didn't listen to reason.

"It's tragic that Kendry died," she said. "But it doesn't mean you have to deny your own Gift. Do you really think he would have wanted that? Or that your family blames you?"

"It's not fair." Edwold looked up at her, guilt shadowing his eyes. "I shouldn't be happy, when he's gone. And I don't want my parents to think I don't care about…what happened."

"Is the anniversary of your brother's death during the Spring Fair festivities?"

He nodded mutely, and Shandara felt another pang for the boy. The Vernal Equinox was supposed to be a time of joyful celebration of all the bonds of love. But maybe, despite the tragedy of his brother's death, she could help Edwold see that act of heroism for what it was.

"Why did Kendry push you out of the way?" she asked.

"To save me." He looked down at the floor.

"Yes—but why?"

"Because he was supposed to watch out for his little brother?" His hands were squeezed together so hard that his knuckles were white.

"Plenty of people are supposed to take care of others, and don't. Kendry made a choice to save you. I think he must have loved you very much."

Edwold sniffed, then glanced up at her. "He shouldn't have."

"Shouldn't have saved you, or shouldn't have loved you?" She tightened her arm around his shoulders. "He did both. Do you think he would have been able to sing, after watching you get crushed by a falling cliff? To go off to Collegium, carrying the knowledge that he'd failed his little brother, failed his family?"

"I..." Edwold pursed his mouth.

Shandara waited, letting him work through the ramifications of her question. Her heart hurt for him, for the whole family, but refusing to shine wasn't the answer to the darkness of sorrow. It never was.

"We both should have lived," the boy finally said.

"Of course you should have." She gave him a sorrowful smile. "But that's a perfect dream of something that didn't happen. Kendry didn't save you so that you could be sad all your life."

Edwold drew in a shaky breath, and then bobbed his head. "I guess...I understand."

"Will you be able to perform the solo, or should we try and find someone else?"

"I think..." He bit his lip. The grief in his expression slowly faded, replaced by worry-tinged resolve. "I think I can do it. I'll try."

"No more tricks to avoid singing?" She raised her brows at him.

A faint smile tugged the corner of his mouth. "They were good ones, though."

She shook her head. "Very creative, I'll give you that. Now, go practice. I'll see you at dress rehearsal."

"Thank you." He leaned in, gave her a squeeze her around the middle, then rose and headed out the door.

Slowly, Shandara finished her tea. She wasn't entirely sure she'd helped Edwold enough—the boy had been carrying a heavy burden, and that couldn't be easy to set down, even taking into account the resiliency of youth.

They'd know soon whether he'd be able to put aside the guilt and sorrow, stand tall, and let his voice ring out. She hoped, for all their sakes, that he was strong enough.

"Is your ensemble ready?" Tarek asked as he and Shandara strode out of the Collegium gates toward the Spring Fair.

"Maybe."

Shandara adjusted the carrying strap of her harp and squinted at the bright pennants hung around the perimeter of the Fair. The day was chilly, but the sunlight carried a welcome warmth—which would help keep the instruments in tune once the Trainee's Ensemble took the stage. One less thing to worry about.

Delicious smells from the food vendors wafted through the air, and the sound of laughter rang over the babble of the crowd. Many of the attendees wore ribbon-bedecked love tokens in their hair or pinned to their clothing, and the mood was merry.

The gaiety only underscored Shandara's anxiety. She hadn't gone into detail with Tarek, but the dress rehearsal had been less-than-ideal.

A bad dress rehearsal means a good performance, she reminded herself, trying to believe the old adage was true.

It wasn't just Edwold's shaky solo that had her concerned, though that was the pinnacle of her worry. He'd had to stop halfway through 'Ode to a Companion,' his voice choked with tears, and his tension had translated to the rest of the ensemble.

Tempos were all over the place, despite Shandara's keeping time at the front of the group. The flutes squawked, the tenors missed their entrance, the altos were flat. The entire rehearsal had been altogether dreadful.

She'd ended it with a bright smile and words of encouragement she didn't quite feel. Especially not at this moment, making her way to the large stage set in the center of the Fair. Her stomach knotted as she saw the members of the Trainee's Ensemble milling about at one side.

"You brought your harp." Tarek nodded to the instrument she carried.

"Yes." Moved by an impulse she didn't quite understand, Shandara had grabbed her lap harp on the way out the door. "We didn't practice with it though, so…" She trailed off in a shrug.

"Don't worry. I know the performance will go wonderfully." Tarek gave her a smile so full of confidence, she didn't have the heart to contradict him.

They reached the stage, and Shandara was surprised to see Lyssa waiting there among the other Trainees. Edwold stood beside her, a shadowed look in his eyes.

"Hello, Lyssa," Shandara said. "Is everything well?"

"I think so." The girl gave her a crooked smile. "I've been talking with Edwold."

Shandara glanced at the boy.

"She said maybe she could help," he said, shuffling his feet. "If you don't mind, Bard Shandara."

"Not at all." Shandara's tension eased down a notch. She wasn't sure what Lyssa might be able to do, but just having the girl there was a relief.

"I told Edwold I'd sensed he was having trouble, during rehearsal," Lyssa said. "With his permission, I'll be standing by to lend my support during the performance. Maybe my Gift will be able to help."

"I hope so," Edwold said fervently. He jerked his chin to the front of the stage. "My family is right there, front and center and I…" His expression folded, and it was clear he was battling back tears.

"I'll be right here," Lyssa said. "You'll do fine."

On stage, Master Bard Tangeli was thanking the previous group of Bards, who had showcased a lively set of dance tunes from the Rethwellan border.

"I know many of you are especially looking forward to the next performance," Master Tangeli said. "The Bardic Collegium is pleased to present the Trainee's Ensemble!"

Amid cheers, the students mounted the low stairs and filed onto the stage. The instrumentalists, including Jaya, took the chairs in the center, while the vocalists ranged behind them. Edwold stood in the front row, his face pale.

Tarek squeezed Shandara's shoulders. "Good luck," he whispered.

She gave him a tight nod, then strode onto the stage. A quick glance into the crowd showed her a dark-haired couple standing up front, with two younger children who bore a marked resemblance to Edwold. They wore cautious smiles, and the littlest girl waved excitedly as she spotted her brother.

Turning to her Trainees, Shandara gave them a heartening smile.

"Let's give them our best," she said, her voice pitched for the ensemble's ears alone. "I know you'll make your families proud."

Her gaze landed on Edwold and he gave her a faint nod. Still, she saw the misgivings in his eyes.

Before the group could give in to their restless nerves, Shandara lifted her hands, nodded to Jaya for the opening notes, and launched them into "The Sparrows Aloft."

Despite a shaky start, the ensemble rallied, and soon the joyful chorus filled the air. Bright trills from the flutes and a lovely run from Jaya's gittern embroidered the melody, and Shandara felt her heart lighten.

The second piece, an instrumental with wordless choral accompaniment, went equally well. The audience applauded and shouted encouragement, and Shandara's smile to the group widened.

But "Ode to a Companion" was next. As the instruments checked their tuning, Shandara watched Edwold with concern. The boy's eyes were shadowed, his face tense.

Shandara pulled her harp from its case and went to sit by Jaya, ostensibly to tune up, but also to be near Edwold.

"You *can* do this," she said to him.

He swallowed and couldn't meet her eyes.

"Ready?" Shandara called to the group. "Follow me from here, please."

The whispering Trainees quieted, the silence spreading in ripples out into the crowd until they sat in the center of a hushed expectancy.

Shandara nodded to Jaya, then joined her on the intro. As her fingers plucked the harp strings, she concentrated on breathing with the music, on infusing the notes with assurance and directing it at Edwold.

The singers entered on cue.

Edwold blinked rapidly, swaying.

"Unlock your knees," Shandara whispered urgently to him. He couldn't pass out now.

The chorus softened, holding their note. Edwold opened his mouth.

No sound emerged.

Sing! Shandara thought at him. *You can, I know you can.*

Still he stood there, paralyzed. Another second more and the piece would fall apart.

Unless...

Hoping the ensemble would follow her, Shandara began to play loudly, ringing the notes of the melody line to give Edwold more time.

There was a stuttering moment as some of the singers followed her, and some didn't. Then the piece settled, and Shandara was suffused with gratitude. No matter how fractious and silly the Trainees could be, they were true musicians at their cores.

Indeed, as she wound the melody around and back to the solo's starting point, the ensemble coalesced, sounding even better than at any point during their practice.

A bit of color returned to Edwold's cheeks.

This time, when they hit his cue, he opened his mouth and sang.

Clear and high, the verse soared above the crowd, telling of the connection between Companion and Herald. The audience listened, riveted, and Shandara sat back in relief.

A relief that was short lived.

Edwold reached the second stanza and shot her a panicked look. Too late, she realized that *this* section was the danger point. The verse about how the bonds of love could transcend even death was next—and Edwold was breaking.

His voice cracked.

He dragged in a fresh breath and tried again, but his voice fell short of the high, soaring melody. In the front row, his parents looked on with stricken expressions.

A faint sense of misery began to permeate the air, and the crowd began to whisper.

Then, suddenly, Lyssa was there. She knelt on the stage before Edwold and grasped his hands.

"Sing," she commanded.

Shandara nodded and played a ringing chord, pulling the fragmented ensemble back onto the beat. They could do this. They *must*.

Desperately, Edwold tried again. This time, a surge of warmth followed. He reached the first note. Then the second.

Shandara could not quite sense Lyssa's outpouring of

confidence and healing, the support that she lent Edwold, but it was there—visible in the straightening of his spine, in the increasing strength of his voice.

Once again, the ensemble rallied. Shandara led with her harp, her voice, keeping the chorus quiet enough that Edwold's solo could soar.

They reached the final verse, and, with searing poignancy, Edwold sang—straight at his family.

Whatever else remains below,
   We carry on, we carry on,
   Remembering what is above.
   We carry on with love.

The music swelled, the final chord holding, holding…until Shandara lifted her hand and swept it to the side. The ensemble cut off perfectly—not a single straggler or missed note.

A moment of awed silence followed.

Shandara looked at Edwold's parents, their faces shining with tears. With approval. With love.

Then the audience broke into riotous cheers and applause. Lyssa slowly rose to stand, her face soft as she looked at Edwold.

"You did it," Shandara said to him—to the whole Trainee's Ensemble. "I'm so proud of you."

She beckoned the boy to step forward and take his well-deserved bow. He did, his eyes bright, his smile wobbly about the edges.

"Thank you," he said to her as he went back to his place.

Lyssa held her hand out to him, and he took it, the gesture all but lost as the other soloist took her bow, and the rest of the ensemble followed suit.

As they left the stage, they were already turning back into rowdy youths. Several of them stopped to congratulate Edwold, some by mussing his hair, others by offering to buy him sweets.

"Thanks, but I'm going with Lyssa to the pie vendor," he said, a wash of pink across his cheeks. "After I see my family."

Edwold's sisters and parents rounded the corner of the stage, and there was no mistaking the gladness in their eyes. His mother went straight to him and enfolded him in her embrace.

"We are so very proud of you," she said. "And I know Kendry would be, too."

Edwold cleared his throat. "I sang it for you. For him."

"We know." His father's voice held a somber note, but his expression was tempered with joy. "You honor his memory."

He leaned over, drawing his whole family into his arms.

Shandara turned away, eyes pricking with tears, to find Tarek waiting for her.

"Nice work, Bard Shandara," he said softly.

"Thank you." She let out a breath. "For everything."

"I bought you this." He held out a white-ribboned token embellished with strands of silver. "It made me think of you—and the brightness you bring into the world."

She did start crying then, as the emotions of the day overtook her. Tarek pulled her into a hug.

"I feel silly," she said, the words muffled into his coat as she leaned into him.

"You can be as silly, or as strong, as you need to, Shan," he said. "No matter what, I'll be here for you."

"I know."

She snuffled a bit more, but the tears passed quickly. By the time she straightened and smiled at Tarek, she was filled with lightness.

"I'll gladly wear your token," she said. "As long as you'll let me buy you one in return."

He smiled down at her, the corners of his eyes crinkling. "Nothing would please me better."

"Ooh," a girl's voice broke in, "does this mean you're handfasted?"

Shandara glanced at Lyssa, who stood just within earshot.

"Don't you have a pie date?" Shandara asked archly. "I noticed you and Edwold holding hands."

Lyssa grinned. "Exchanging pocket pies doesn't mean anything. Not like *love* tokens."

Tarek swatted at her, and she nimbly danced to the side, then went to join Edwold and his family.

Shandara watched her go, with a fond shake of her head.

"I could use a bite to eat," she said, turning back to Tarek. "Let me just tuck my harp away."

"Then we shall wander the Fair together." He extended his arm. "My lady?"

She made him a curtsy, then threaded her elbow through his. "Indeed, my lord. Indeed."

~*~

THE SALT PRINCESS

CHAPTER 1

THE FIRST LIGHT of dawn lay soft over the hills outside Castle Clare, but the forest shadows still held the cool breath of night. Brianne O'Leary made her careful way through the underbrush, her green woolen cloak wrapped tightly about her, the hem dark with dew. Declan waited for her in the clearing where the ancient oak tree grew, and her heart sped at the thought of him.

In the charcoal darkness before sunrise, she'd crept from her room in the bower, where she slept with her two older sisters, and slipped out of the castle. Past the slumbering guard at the gate - and wouldn't her father, the king, have stern words if he were to hear of that dereliction of duty - past the fields and farms, and finally into the sheltering woods. It was the only place she could meet with Declan, away from prying eyes and wagging tongues. For he was a miller's son, and she was a princess, and her father would never allow them to wed.

Indeed, the king was in the midst of arranging marriages for all three of his daughters. Advantageous matches with neighboring lords that would cement his power in the west. Brianne had told him she had no desire to marry Lord Inchiquin, who was nearly twice her age, but the king had only laughed and waved his hand.

"It's not for you to choose, daughter," he said.

"But I don't care for him. His breath smells of old cheese." Brianne prided herself on always telling the truth, though her older sisters had scolded her for it more often than not.

"Must you be so blunt?" Colleen had said, when Brianne told her that her new gown was unflattering.

"It's insulting," Eva had agreed. "Just because we ask for your opinion doesn't mean you have to answer so rudely."

"If you don't want to hear the truth, then don't ask," Brianne had said, a touch indignantly. "I won't be lying to spare your feelings."

Ever since their mother had died - although the king had assured his daughters the queen was going to recover from her illness - Brianne had no taste for sweet untruths. She far preferred the straightforward to the circuitous. Even if it angered her sisters.

"I'll forgive you," Colleen said, tossing her dark plait over her shoulder, "but only if you help make supper tonight."

Brianne lifted one eyebrow. It was true that she'd a Talent for cookery, and she enjoyed her time in the kitchen, but she disliked the extortion.

"I will, at that," she said. "Though not because you ask. Forgive me, or not, I don't care."

In fact, the hunters had brought in a brace of hares, and she had a rabbit stew recipe she was eager to try. The cook was happy for Brianne's help, and the warm kitchen of Castle Clare was where Brianne felt closest to the memory of her mother. The queen had taught her how to bake and blend, fillet and fry, season and salt. She'd had a rare magic that way, too.

Indeed, like their mother, each of the princesses had a touch of the old Gifts. Brianne's affinity for cooking went far beyond the usual, her dishes flavorful and unique even when she only had the most ordinary ingredients at hand.

Colleen had a way with metal, able to polish up silver with the simple swipe of a rag, or find any lost coins that had rolled away. Once a month she spent the day in the local smithy, where the blacksmiths swore they were able to work three times faster and turn out higher-quality work than without her presence.

Eva's water empathy was useful, as well. She was in demand as a dowser when the farmers wanted to dig a new well, and her bath water almost never went cold, no matter how long she chose to stay in the large tub they used for bathing.

The king was pleased that his daughters had such useful skills, although right after the queen's death, Brianne had been banished from the kitchen for over-salting the food with her tears.

Her grief had become more manageable over time. But the second anniversary of the queen's death was fast approaching, sending a shadow of memory over the inhabitants of the castle. Still, Brianne's blossoming relationship with Declan had reminded her that happiness existed in the world, too, hand-in-hand with sorrow.

She'd gone to the mill for a special sack of finely ground barley flour and ended up spending nearly an hour talking with the miller's handsome son. For nearly a year now, they'd snuck out to meet one another in the forest, though Declan's duties at the mill were taking up more and more of his time.

He was waiting for her beneath the oak, his brown hair the glossy color of ripe chestnuts, his hazel eyes like midsummer leaves, his smile warmer than the fire upon the great hearth of the castle. Brianne's heart gave a thump of joy at the sight of him.

"Declan," she called, and ran across the damp grasses to be folded into his embrace.

He held her close for a moment, their hearts beating in one rhythm, then brushed his lips over hers in a kiss that held a touch of melancholy.

"What is it?" She stepped back and searched his eyes.

"I am traveling to Dublin with my father," he said.

It was a journey of well over a week, and her joy faded. "Must you go?"

"Aye. The new burrstones have arrived from England, and he wants me to meet with the importer and stonemasons, so that I might deal properly with them in the future."

"It's a dangerous journey." Her fingers tightened on Declan's arm. "The brigands are bold upon the highway this year."

"My father is hiring two guardsmen. With them along, I've no doubt we'll arrive safely."

Brianne dredged up a smile. "Then I'm glad your father is taking precautions. But please take care. I couldn't bear to lose you."

"Don't worry, beloved." He brushed another kiss across her lips. "I'll return as soon as I may."

She nodded, her throat tight with tears. There was no stopping him. Even if they had been able to court openly, he still would have to go. And in truth, their meetings must remain secret until they convinced the village priest to marry them. Thus far, the priest had refused to do any such thing, for fear of angering the king and losing his position. Rightly so, of course, but the knowledge was bitter.

"Come home safe to me," she said to Declan. "I'll try to convince my father to change his mind during your absence. Perhaps when you return, he'll give us his blessing."

"Perhaps." Declan's expression was doubtful.

Brianne bit her tongue on the argument that they could run away together. They'd discussed it before, in a brief and shining burst of hope. But then Declan shook his head and reminded her that he couldn't abandon his family. He was the only son, and the business would fall upon his shoulders soon enough.

He was a steady, honest man who would never abandon his responsibilities. It was one of the things she loved about him, after all. He would never lie to her to spare her feelings.

She let out a low breath. Yet no matter how true and deep their love, it was entirely possible that they would not be able to marry, nor spend their lives together.

The knowledge twisted in her like a knife, but it was better than the slow poison of lies. So she held him close, and kissed him again, and they spoke of it no more.

Declan and his father departed for Dublin. His absence, along with the fast-approaching anniversary of her mother's death, turned Brianne's mood melancholy.

Well then, she told herself sternly, tired of her own moping about, *do something*.

There could be no changing the fact that the queen was gone. Brianne might be motherless, but that didn't mean she must drift aimlessly in the current of life. It was high time she speak with her father again about Lord Inchiquin - and her staunch refusal to marry the fellow.

The king had brushed her words away the last time. But if she made it clear how very *serious* she was in her opposition to the match, perhaps he'd relent.

And then she and Declan could be married.

Fortified with hope, Brianne went to her father's study the next morning. He and his seneschal were going over the farmers' tallies, but when Brianne knocked, the king dismissed his man and beckoned for her to enter.

"I brought you a bit of something to eat," she said, setting down the tray she'd carried up from the kitchen.

She'd baked a dozen buttery scones, filled with currants and honey to sweeten his mood, and brewed a nice strong tisane of herbs to go with them.

"Thank you, daughter," the king said, smiling as he lifted a scone from the plate. "I can see you've something you wish to discuss. Are you ready to take Lord Inchiquin's suit seriously?"

Not a good beginning. Brianne knotted her hands in her apron.

"I *do* want to speak with you regarding Lord Inchiquin…" She trailed off, waiting for her father to take a bite of the pastry.

To her relief, he did, nodding with satisfaction. "Delicious, as ever. Do go on."

"Well. I told you I wouldn't marry him."

"That you did." The king smiled indulgently and continued eating his scone.

"And I meant it." She straightened and met her father's gaze. "You've two other daughters to do your bidding, but I refuse."

The king's expression darkened with anger. Slowly, he set down the half-eaten scone.

"*All* of my daughters will do my bidding." His voice was hard. "Which includes marrying the lord I've selected for them. It's for your own good, as well as that of the kingdom."

"It's not!" she cried, her dreams withering like flowers in a sudden frost. "What if I love another?"

"Who?" The king's gaze bored into hers, wrath sparking in his eyes. "What lordling thinks to win your hand without my approval?"

"There is no lordling," she hurried to say, though her heart quailed. Despite her insistence on the truth, she hadn't enough courage to tell her father who it was she truly loved.

Such a confession could only place Declan and his entire family in danger. The king could turn them all out of their home, command the mill to be handed over to some other family, and chase them beyond the borders of Clare. All because the miller's son had the temerity to fall in love with a princess.

She couldn't bring such a fate upon them. Brianne swallowed the bitterness of her truth, and faced her father unflinchingly.

"But there might be, some day," she said. "And what then? I'll not be shackled to a man I cannot love, nor will I make a cuckold of him. Will you doom your daughter to such a miserable existence?"

"Enough!" The force of the king's voice shook the mug upon the tray, the untouched liquid trembling. "You are young, and know nothing of life. I'll hear no more of this. And you're banished to your room until tomorrow."

Brianne clenched her jaw and whirled for the door. Tears stinging her eyes, she stalked to the bower room in the turret.

Eva was there, braiding her long hair, so Brianne didn't even have the privacy to fling herself down upon her bed and give in to the storm of weeping roiling through her.

"What's the matter?" her sister asked, looking up from the dressing table they shared.

"Father's commanded me to stay up here until tomorrow."

"What did you do?" Eva turned fully around and studied Brianne closely. "Did you try and tell him you won't marry Lord Inchiquin again?"

Brianne picked up her pillow and clutched it to her chest. "I thought this time he'd listen."

"Oh, Bri." Eva shook her head. "He's too stubborn for argument. You'll have to bring him around more subtly."

"I baked scones."

"Even your marvelous cooking skills aren't enough to change someone's mind when they're set on a thing. You should have asked me and Colleen for help."

Brianne grimaced. Eva was right, she *should* have waited, should've enlisted her sisters' aid. But she'd been so sure, the hope in her heart so strong…

She let out a heavy sigh and sank down on her bed. "What do I do, now?"

"Be patient. We're all on edge these days. Give him until after the morrow."

Brianne nodded grimly. In hindsight, the day before the anniversary of the queen's death hadn't been the right time to try and sweeten her father. But she'd *so* wanted to give Declan good news when he returned.

Instead, she'd only hardened the barriers standing in their way.

"I'll spend all day tomorrow cooking," she said.

Maybe serving an elaborate feast would help make amends between herself and the king. At any rate, it would distract her from the current bog she was wading through.

Eva gave her a wry look. "Just don't cry in the food, all right? We want the meal to be edible."

Brianne wrinkled her nose at her sister, but she felt better. Eva was right; once they moved past the difficult day ahead, surely her father would listen to reason.

CHAPTER 2

BRIANNE WOKE the next morning already thinking of what she planned to make for dinner. She hurried down to the kitchens to consult with the cook, and they quickly set to work. The scullery maid started scrubbing up vegetables, while Brianne went through the spice chest and the cook fetched butter and cream from the cool-room.

The day flew by, the heat of the ovens and cooking fire baking all the misery out of Brianne's body until there was only the simple dance of chop and stir, sip and season.

Finally, the cook chased her from the kitchen, admonishing her to go put on a new gown before dinner - one not dusted with flour and spotted with oil.

As most of the cooking was done, Brianne obeyed. She chose a dark blue dress with a touch of embroidery on the bodice and sleeves. Somber, to honor their grief. But from the trunk at the end of her bed she pulled a red woolen shawl. It had belonged to her mother, and Brianne folded that brightness about her shoulders, a reminder that life went on. Her mother wouldn't want her family to be mired in sorrow forever.

The fire on the great hearth was lit and the castle's two tall golden candelabra shed light over the table as the family gathered for the meal.

The king took his usual place at the head of the table, where a cup of mead awaited. The candlelight sparked golden glints from the circlet about his brow, and picked out the new lines upon his weathered face. With a pang, Brianne realized her father was growing old. No wonder he wanted to secure good matches for his daughters, to make sure the castle passed to a man of high birth.

Although, as the youngest, it wasn't fair that Brianne was expected to marry a nobleman, too. But now was not the time to turn about in her own self-pity. Brianne shook her selfish thoughts away and smiled at her sisters; Colleen at her father's right hand, Eva beside her on the left.

"You're in a fine mood," Eva said. "I expect a delicious feast, judging from the light in your eyes."

"It will be, at that."

They began with a tureen of leek soup, followed by bread baked with the miller's best flour. The taste of it reminded Brianne of Declan, and she hoped he and his father had reached Dublin safely and concluded their business. Even now, they could be on the road home.

"This is wonderful," her father said, taking a bite of roasted pheasant stuffed with buttered turnips. "Did you add a new herb?"

"I did, thank you. There's a bit of tarragon in the sauce, along with sage and thyme."

"Perfectly seasoned." He brandished his fork in approval

before proceeding to eat every last bite on his plate.

The servants kept his mead cup filled, and as the meal progressed his manner grew softer toward his daughters. Brianne credited her cooking, of course, but the constant flow of alcohol certainly didn't hurt. She was glad the anniversary was proving less painful than the previous year, when - despite her best efforts - they'd had a grim and woeful meal, and then all gone to bed early.

After the pheasant came braised rabbits served over fresh greens, and then a final subtlety to finish the meal with a bit of sweetness. Brianne had whipped eggs into a meringue and fashioned a posy of edible flowers. She'd studded the bouquet with plums and gooseberries, then dusted it with a precious bit of nutmeg she'd been hoarding in the spice chest.

Replete, the family sat back in their chairs. The king smiled fondly at his daughters.

"Your mother would be so proud to see what fine young women you've grown into," he said. ""I do love you, children of my heart."

"We love you, too," Colleen said.

The king nodded, a teasing light in his eyes. "Ah, but how much, my eldest girl?"

He awaited her answer with a smile.

After a moment's thought, Colleen smiled back at him. "I love you as much as all the gold in the land."

"A fine answer." He nodded, clearly pleased. "And what of you, Eva?"

Eva pursed her lips, then gave her answer. "I love you as much as the oceans are wide."

"A vast amount, indeed!" He laughed and patted her arm. "Brianne, can you come up with anything better?"

For a fleeting moment, Brianne considered proclaiming some grandiose affection, like all the stars in the sky or blades of grass in the kingdom. But in truth those were foolish things, and she didn't truly *love* them. They weren't essential. Not the way family was.

She met her father's gaze. "I love you as much as salt."

"Salt?" His smile fell and his gray eyes grew cold. "Did I hear you aright, daughter? You love me as much as *salt?*"

"Yes." She swallowed back the sudden knowledge that she'd answered too honestly, too bluntly.

The king wanted lavish things, like gold and seas and stars. Salt was too small. Too common - even though its lack in the kitchen would be disastrous.

Eva turned to her, frowning. "That's a foolish answer. Perhaps you've a better reply to our father?"

Brianne scowled back. If her family couldn't see how important, how *vital*, her answer had been, it was no fault of her own.

"Salt is my answer," she said stubbornly. "And salt it will remain."

"Ungrateful girl!" The king stood, scraping his chair back. His cheeks were flushed with temper. "First you argue with me over marrying, and now to say such a thing in front of your sisters. I'd thought you cared a bit better for me, Brianne. Such a paltry answer insults me. Insults all of us, and particularly the memory of your mother."

"But father - "

"Silence!" There was a wild light in his eyes, brought forth by grief and anger. "If you persist in arguing with me then perhaps you should spend a fortnight sleeping the forest, until you come to your senses."

Her sisters exchanged worried glances, and Brianne tried once more to explain.

"I only meant - "

"There are no words you can say that will undo this. Go." He pointed to the door, his expression dark. "Gather up whatever supplies you can carry, and don't come back until you've an apology upon your lips and are ready to accept Lord Inchiquin as your husband."

Colleen inhaled and sent Brianne a beseeching look. Eva tried to catch her hand, but Brianne ignored her sisters. Very well. If this were the truth of her family, of her father, then she would accept it.

Lips pinched together, half in anger, half to hold back her tears, she stood. "I'll gladly go live in the woods for *years*, if it means I won't have to marry that doddering old lord. And if you're too foolish to understand how much I love you, then that's upon your head. Not mine."

Vision blurring, she whirled and stalked quickly to the door. She'd take what she needed to survive, and nothing more.

"Wait," Colleen cried, but the king's voice overrode hers.

"I meant what I said, daughter," he called after her. "No need to show your face until you've an apology in one hand and obedience in the other."

That will never happen, Brianne thought fiercely back at him. Her pride and anger kept her marching forward, unspeaking. She would take her refuge in the forest, even as frost turned the leaves brown and sharpened the night stars with ice.

But she would never tell a sweet lie to soothe her father's temper. No matter the cost.

CHAPTER 3

BRIANNE'S first few days in the forest passed well enough. She constructed a rude shelter of boughs over a nest of rushes, and spent the nights there warm, wrapped in her woolen cloak with her mother's red shawl for a pillow.

Her camp was near a small stream, far enough from the water's edge to not disturb the creatures that drank from its clear current, but close enough that she could fetch water to boil and cook with. She had flint and tinder, a cooking pot, and the sharp dagger at her belt - enough items for a rudimentary kitchen. In addition to an extra set of clothing and her single blanket, she'd had the foresight to bring a length of wire to fashion snares with. She wouldn't go hungry.

Berries hung ripe on the bushes, and there were nuts to glean and cattail tubers to harvest. She found a small patch of wild onions, and managed to catch a hare in one of her snares. And, of course, she'd brought a jar of salt from the castle.

As she sprinkled it into her rabbit stew, her mouth twisted bitterly. Ah, if her father could only taste a meal made *without* salt, then surely he'd change his tune. But even though the cook was her ally and friend, not a one of the servants would allow her to sneak back into the castle to try to prove her point.

The king's word was law, after all.

By the end of the first week, the fall winds were beginning to blow, bringing storms across the land. Brianne's cookfire went out and she'd no dry kindling. She spent a miserable few days huddled in her dripping shelter, eating raw mushrooms and berries and wishing for the sun and Declan's return.

Not to mention the company of her sisters, her soft bed in the castle, the warmth of the fire upon the hearth…

Still, she'd no intention of groveling for the king's approval. And even less taste for the thought of wedding herself to Lord Inchiquin. Better a few uncomfortable weeks in the forest than a lifetime of unhappiness.

Declan would be home any day, surely. And now that the king had cast his youngest daughter out, the village priest must see reason. If all went well, she and Declan could be wed before the last leaves fell from the oaks.

She clung to that hope, even as the days passed. The air grew colder and the leaves abandoned the trees.

Declan, she whispered into the rising sun. *Where are you?*

The berries withered, the last nuts taken by squirrels, and the land settled in for winter. Brianne punched a new hole in her belt to cinch it tighter about her waist. And then another.

She waited beneath the ancient oak, and crept to the verge of the forest, keeping watch. A week passed, and then another, and still her true love did not come.

Finally, she knew she must go in search of him.

She combed the worst of the tangles from her hair, scrubbed herself in the stream, gasping with cold, and donned her spare gown. She'd been saving it for when Declan returned, and was dismayed at how loosely it hung from her shoulders.

At least it was clean, even if it no longer fit. Her blue dress was stained and torn, despite her best efforts. Living for weeks in the forest, it was impossible to avoid smears of berries and lichens, snags from thorns and brambles, mud ground into the skirt. Her cloak was not in much better condition, but it warded off the cold well enough, despite its stains and tatters.

Ready to face the world, she bundled her few possessions into the red shawl and headed for the village. She'd barely set foot past the first few cottages, when one of the baker's boys spotted her.

"Oi, beggar woman," he called. "You can have a bit of bread from my father, if you'll be on your way, after."

Brianne nodded, her stomach knotting at the thought of fresh-baked bread as she followed the lad to the baker's door. There was no point in trying to convince the boy of her true identity, but surely the baker would recognize her.

To her shock, he did not, only handed her the end of a loaf and told her to go.

"Wait," she said, tucking the bread away though her hands trembled with the desire to tear into it straightway, "I'm looking for Declan, the miller's son."

The baker frowned. "We all are, and for his father, too. The flour's not what it was, I'm sad to say, but we make the best of it."

Fear rippled through her. "What happened to them?"

"They went off to Dublin, nigh on two months ago, and no one has seen or heard from them since." He shook his head sadly. "Must have been brigands upon the road. His wife is carrying on as best she can, but when spring comes, she'll be selling the mill. Aye, but that's enough village gossip. You've your bread. Now be off."

Her heart as heavy as a stone, Brianne trudged past the village green to the crossroads.

She'd no money. No food but a few dried berries and mushrooms and the heel of a loaf of bread. But she had her wits, a sharp dagger, and a good woolen cloak. That would have to be enough.

She paused, glanced back at the silhouette of the castle in the far distance, then turned her feet toward Dublin. Though it might be a hopeless task, she would go in search of her true love.

CHAPTER 4

BRIANNE'S BOOTS sank into the mud of the road. The constant drizzle weighed down her woolen cloak until it felt as if it were made of iron, but she bowed her head and kept on. When she could no longer ignore the pangs of hunger in her stomach, she took shelter beneath a dripping holly tree and brought out her bread.

The crust was thick and hard to bite through, the texture of the bread heavy. Somehow, it managed to be both dry and soggy at the same time. She held the heel up and inspected it, realizing the flour was so unevenly ground as to have rendered the dough like paste in some places and like coarse sand in others.

The millstones clearly needed balancing. Where were Declan and his father?

I'll find you, she promised, sending her thoughts winging beneath the gray sky.

Meanwhile, she had an inedible piece of bread to make palatable. She cast about for two flat stones, then pulled out her bark-wrapped packet of dried berries. A few hardy stalks of wild anise grew beside the road, and she plucked a handful to add sweetness and flavor.

She crumbled the bread - not the easiest task - onto one of the flat stones and added the berries and anise, along with a bit of water from her waterskin. Humming, for the act of making food always cheered her, no matter how simple the ingredients, she began grinding and smashing everything together.

As she worked, she kept her mind turned to happy things: the sun upon her face, the laughter of her sisters, Declan's kisses…

After a short time she had a purplish dough, infused with fortitude and hope. She formed it into three balls, then pressed each one flat into a cake. They'd be best fried over a fire, and second-best left to dry, but she was hungry and ate one of them right away.

It didn't taste terrible, although the consistency was a bit chewy. As she swallowed the last bite, she felt her mood lift. Surely this journey would end in success. She carefully tucked the remaining two cakes into the bark wrapper she'd used to store her berries, then set off once again.

The rain had stopped, and her steps were lighter along the road. She skirted the worst of the puddles and walked on, keeping herself occupied by recalling every detail of Declan's face. Memories of their time together accompanied her until dusk began to shadow the sky.

Belatedly, she looked about for a place to spend the night. She'd passed a few small villages and farmsteads, but there was nothing but open countryside around her now. With a sigh she resigned herself to a night spent wrapped in her soggy cloak beneath a gorse bush.

She was just about to turn off the roadway when she spotted two travelers coming toward her. *Brigands!* Her hand went to the knife at her belt, but her fear quickly faded as she saw that one of the men was limping badly, supported by his companion.

There was something familiar in the younger man's way of walking. Brianne's heart gave a huge thump, and then she picked up her skirts in both hands and began to run. She splashed recklessly through the puddles, and nearly lost her footing in a patch of mud, but the hope in her chest pushed her on.

"Declan," she gasped when she finally drew close enough to make out his features.

The tightness in her chest made it impossible for her to say more. Their gazes met, and the love and relief in his eyes told her there were no words necessary.

At that moment, the old miller let out a cry and pitched forward. Declan barely caught him, and Brianne leapt forward to help keep the old man from tumbling face-first into the mud.

"Father?" Declan asked as the miller hung limply in his arms.

There was no response, and Declan gave her a panicked look.

"He still breathes," she said. "There - his chest is rising and falling."

Between them, they got the old man to the side of the road and propped his back against a stone, but he still did not awaken.

"He is weak from his injury, and hunger," Declan said.

"I've a bite." Hastily, Brianne pulled out one of her berry cakes and her flask of clear water.

The first piece tumbled from the miller's lips, and Brianne felt despair touch her soul. But Declan coaxed a bit of water into his father's mouth, and the man roused enough to chew and swallow.

"You must eat some, too," she said to Declan. "The village is still a long day's journey away." And that was on two strong legs.

He shook his head. "I'll save the rest for him."

"I've another cake. Take a bite or two, at least."

He did, and a hint of color returned to his cheeks, though he still insisted on feeding most of the cake to his father. Finally, the old man opened his eyes. His gaze went from Declan to Brianne, and he squinted at her.

"What beggar woman is this?" His voice was hoarse. "We've no coin for you, and no food. I'm sorry lass, but our own journey has been a hard one and we've naught to spare."

"Father," Declan said, "do you not recognize Princess Brianne?"

The miller let out a snort and managed to sit up a bit straighter. "That's no more a princess than I am Lord Mayor of Dublin."

Declan looked at her in turn. "Indeed, there's some truth to my father's words. What has happened to you?"

"A great deal." She reached for his hand, lacing her fingers with his, and told them of her banishment from the castle.

"Stubborn girl," the miller said gruffly when she finished her tale. "Who would be so foolish as to throw away the life of a princess? And over what?"

"Over love," she said, sharing a smile with Declan. Now

that he'd returned, all her sorrow had fled. "But what happened to the two of you? What of the burrstones, and why were you so long away?"

"The stones will be along as soon as the roads dry. But after we arranged transport, I was injured in Dublin. It delayed our return." The miller gestured to his leg, propped before him on the sodden grasses.

"You nearly died after a careless English lord trampled you beneath his horse," Declan said, his voice hot. "That is no small thing. And I still say we should have waited until you were fully healed before we set forth."

His father grunted. "I won't heal better than this, lad. Time you faced the truth."

"Perhaps, but that's no excuse for pushing yourself past the end of your strength."

"I feel much better now," the miller said. "That bit of food revived me more than I thought possible."

Brianne gave him a gentle smile. "I'm pleased to hear it. And glad beyond words that the two of you have returned."

"I'm sorry I couldn't send word to the castle." Declan brushed his fingers over her cheek. "I did ask my sisters to tell you what had happened, though, and why we were late in coming."

"Your messages went astray," she said, her heart turning over at the thought of all the sorrow their family had suffered. "They believe you dead upon the road."

"Then we must make haste home." The miller tried to struggle to his feet, but Declan set a restraining hand upon his shoulder.

"Night is falling, and the road's treacherous. We'll wait until morning."

The miller sighed heavily but made no further argument. Accordingly, Declan scouted a short distance from the roadway until he found a thicket for them to shelter beneath.

And if, in the star-dusted night, Brianne and Declan held hands and traded soft kisses, the snoring miller was none the wiser.

CHAPTER 5

IN THE MORNING, they broke their fast with the last of Brianne's cakes. The little meal sustained them most of the day, though the miller slowed as the sun began to set, his face twisted in pain. Declan supported him on one side, Brianne on the other as they made their halting way down the muddy track.

It was well past sunset by the time the exhausted trio stumbled into the village. The miller was at the end of his strength, and Brianne and Declan were not much better. They barely managed to get to the pub, the nearest building to the road in the whole village.

The moment they stepped through the door, an excited babble arose.

"It that the miller, himself?" someone cried.

"Looks to be," another man said. "And worse for the wear, too."

The publican hurried over, full of concern as he helped them to the nearest table.

"We never thought we'd see you again," he said. "What happened to you in Dublin?"

"I've only the strength for a single telling," Declan said. "Could you bring us stew and ale, and send one of your boys to fetch my mother?"

"Aye." Their host turned back to the kitchen.

With a sigh, the miller set his arms on the table and laid his head down. "Home. At last."

"We couldn't have done it without Brianne." Declan caught her hand, warmth shining from his eyes. "I've waited too long to say this, my love. But will you agree to marry me?"

His words banished Brianne's exhaustion, her heart leaping up like a doe over the meadows.

"That I will, Declan. With all my love."

The nearby patrons let out a cheer, then had to explain to the rest of the room what had just happened. Everyone came over to clap Declan on the back and take a look at this stranger he'd just asked to marry him. Their curiosity turned to surprise when they saw it was the banished princess, but no one begrudged Declan his bride. Who wouldn't want to marry a princess who'd saved your life, after all?

The stew and ale arrived, and the miller's wife and daughters, too. While they ate, Declan told the villagers what had happened, and how Brianne had found them upon the road in the nick of time.

"I understand you're joining our family," the miller's wife said to Brianne with a smile. "I fear our humble house isn't what you're used to, but I bid you warm welcome as a daughter."

Her words pricked tears at the corners of Brianne's eyes. "I care not for living in luxury, as long as I'm with the man I love. And I'll be glad of your mothering hand into the bargain."

It was settled that the priest would marry them in two weeks' time.

"Should we invite the king and your sisters?" Declan asked, giving Brianne a worried look.

"We shall," she said. "Though it might be better not to say who it is you're marrying."

The publican's brows drew together. "I'd not want to bring the wrath of the king down upon us. Are you sure that asking him to the wedding is the wise thing to do?"

"I'll wear a veil," she said, then raised her voice and glanced about the pub. "I promise that the king will welcome me back with open arms, once the wedding feast has begun. But until then, we'll need to keep my identity a secret. Can I rely upon everyone in the village to help?"

"As long as we have edible bread once more, we'd even ride into battle for you," someone called with good humor.

"Too bad you can't ride, Liam," one of his companions replied.

"Or wield a sword," another said, but in the end, everyone promised to keep Brianne's secret.

The evening ended with numerous toasts, and a boisterous escort back to the miller's house, where he was tucked carefully into bed with the doctor's supervision. Despite Brianne's protests, the miller's wife made her daughters all move into one bedroom so that Brianne might have a room of her own.

"Truly, I don't mind sharing," she said, but Declan's mother would hear nothing of it.

"Enjoy your privacy," the miller's wife said. "You'll be

sharing it with Declan soon enough." She winked, and Brianne blushed and argued no more.

The day of the wedding dawned clear, though one glance at the sky told Brianne it would rain later that afternoon. No matter, for the wedding feast would be held at the pub, with all the tables pushed together in the center of the room and more chairs added along the sides.

She'd spent the last three days preparing the food for the wedding feast. The miller's wife had helped a great deal, and between her kitchen and the one at the pub, everything was at the ready.

"I can scarcely wait to eat it," Declan's youngest sister said, clasping her hands eagerly beneath her chin. "It all looks and smells so delicious."

"Out of the kitchen." Her mother flapped her apron, and with a grin the girl scurried away, though she stole a biscuit as she went.

Brianne surveyed the plates of food and smiled. She'd put her utmost into every dish: the roast meats, the pastries, the pies and vegetables. Everything was exquisitely flavored, if she said so herself. Everything, that was, except one specially prepared meal she'd set aside.

"Let's fix your hair and get you gowned," the miller's wife said, wiping a smudge of flour off Brianne's cheek. "Ah, the first of my girls to be married."

They went into the bedroom, and Brianne donned her blue dress. The miller's wife had helped her take it in, though it still fit a bit too loosely. Luckily, two weeks of good food had softened the jut of her hips and wrists, returned the luster to her hair. And a bit of healing magic infused into her meals hadn't hurt any of them.

Indeed, despite his somber predictions, the miller was able to move about with just a cane for help, and the grim hollows in Declan's cheeks were gone, as was the desperation in his eyes. The burrstones were due to be delivered later that week, and all was settling well in the world, as far as he was concerned.

Brianne bit her lip, thinking of the risk she was taking. Would she be able to win back her father's favor? More than just her own happiness depended on it now. The fate of the entire village was at stake, since they'd taken her in, helped her plan this subterfuge.

It was in fate's hands now. She would marry, and feast, and hope for the best.

Once Brianne was dressed, Declan's mother helped braid and coil her hair atop her head, then affix the lace veil.

"Thank you." Brianne stroked the fine lacework. The veil was like frost upon a lake: intricate enough to hide her features, while still allowing her to see out.

"Made with my mother's own hands," the miller's wife said. "I'm glad you're wearing it."

She kissed the top of Brianne's head, just as the church bells began to ring, summoning everyone to the wedding.

CHAPTER 6

THE KING and his daughters sat in the front row of pews.

Brianne looked at the backs of their heads, ringed with crowns of gold and silver, and felt a clutch of fear. So much could go wrong!

If her father recognized her, he could put a stop to the wedding at once and wreak his vengeance upon the villagers.

He will not, she reassured herself. Her form and features had changed, albeit subtly, and she must trust the lace veil to do the rest.

Besides, the king would never expect his daughter to be marrying the miller's son.

With a deep breath, Brianne gathered her courage and paced to the front of the church to stand beside her beloved. As she passed the front pew, she heard her sister Colleen inhale sharply, and her sister Eva say *sh* in an almost imperceptible whisper.

So. Her sisters knew her. Despite the danger, the knowledge warmed Brianne. They, at least, had recognized her.

The ceremony began, and all went well until it was time for Declan to put the ring on her hand. Perhaps made clumsy by the fact of the king sitting in the front row, Declan fumbled with the plain silver band. He dropped it. It fell to the wooden floor and rolled to a stop at Princess Colleen's feet.

The villagers whispered, but Colleen bent and scooped the ring up. She closed her fingers over it and murmured softly, and when she handed it back to Declan, it was shining gold. Through the lace veil, Brianne met her sister's gaze. Colleen winked at her, ever so slightly.

Declan slipped the band upon her finger, and Briane felt her sister's love enfolding her.

At the end of the vows given and received, they drank the ceremonial cups of wine and water. This time, it was the priest's turn to let his nerves overcome him. He managed the wine well enough, but most of the water sloshed out of the small goblet as he handed it to Brianne to drink.

She paused, inclining the nearly empty cup toward Princess Eva. With a slight smile, Eva waved her fingers and the goblet was suddenly full again. Brianne took a sip of the cool, clear liquid. It tingled pleasantly against her lips, and when she swallowed she knew she drank of her sister's benediction, as well.

Now she only needed her father's blessing.

The couple kissed and went down the aisle to the hearty cheers of the villagers. Despite the winter rains, it was a merry procession down to the pub. They went slowly, in consideration of the miller's leg, and so that the miller's wife and daughters could hurry ahead and make sure all was in readiness for the wedding feast.

The king and the princesses rode at the back of the procession, and Brianne was glad of the reprieve. Nervous, too; for the moment of truth would soon be at hand. What if her plan didn't succeed? What if the king didn't forgive her, after all?

He must, she told herself.

Still, when they reached the pub she hastened to ensure that the meal she'd specially prepared for the king was set aside - ready to be served to him, and him alone.

She returned to Declan's side just as the king was congratulating him, not only on his new bride, but his safe return from Dublin.

"And warm wishes to your bride, as well," the king said, turning to her.

"Your majesty." Brianne curtsied, keeping her voice pitched voice low. "Thank you for attending our wedding."

"It is our pleasure," he said, then gave her a penetrating look, as if he could see through the lace obscuring her features. "There is something familiar about you."

"My wife has lived here all her life," Declan said hastily. "She used to serve in the castle."

Brianne resisted the urge to step on his foot to silence him. The conversation was veering into dangerous territory.

"Declan, show the king to his place," she said softly.

"Yes." Colleen stepped up, taking their father's arm and gently tugging him away from Brianne. "Doesn't the food smell wonderful?"

Eva gave her a pointed look as she passed. "I'm certain everything will be delicious."

Declan showed the king and princesses to the head table,

and Brianne went to tell the miller's wife they were ready. Satisfied, she returned to take her place beside Declan. The tables were arranged in such a way that she could watch her father eat without being in his direct line of sight, and as the feast began, she kept a covert eye on him.

The first course was a soup made of wild onions and mushrooms, accompanied by hearth-baked bread made from the miller's best flour and sprinkled with toasted millet. Brianne watched her father eat. As everyone around him happily spooned up their soup, he took a few mouthfuls then, brow furrowed, set his spoon down.

He picked up his bread, took a bite, then, frowning, lifted it to his face and gave it a sniff. Then, with a grunt he put it back on the plate. Next, he turned to his mead, but Brianne had made sure to water down the pitcher he'd be served from. She wanted her father sober.

The next course was braised eels in a savory sauce, accompanied by roast turnips and carrots. Again, as the people around him ate, the king merely picked at his food. Brianne saw her sisters notice that their father was barely eating, and they began to loudly praise the food, exclaiming over how delicious it was. The king's expression grew darker.

The third course was venison - one of the king's favorite dishes. Although the dish served to him was tender and looked marvelous, Brianne had taken special care with it.

Grimly, the king took a bite. He glanced at his daughters, who were once again remarking on how wonderful it was.

"Enough!" he cried. "What is wrong with my food?"

"What are you saying?" Colleen gave him an innocent look. "It's one of the best meals I've had in quite some time."

"I agree," said Eva, shooting a glance across the room to where Brianne sat. "The flavors are magnificent."

"No, they are not. I can tell the food is spiced, and yet, it is tasteless." The king gestured at his venison. "Even this! I don't understand."

"I do." Brianne stood and lifted her veil. "None of your food contains salt."

"Brianne?" The king rose, peering at her. "You are the bride?"

"I am." She lifted her chin. "And the cook."

Her father glanced down at his plate, then reached over and snagged a bite of venison from Colleen's. The entire room watched in quiet fascination as he chewed, eyes closed.

"Ah," he said. "Delicious. I think I understand."

Brianne swayed, her legs going weak with relief. Declan stood, slipping his arm about her waist to keep her steady. Still, she had to make sure.

"Do you, father?" she asked. "Do you truly know what I meant when I said I loved you as much as salt?"

He paused, looking down at the food before him, then back to Brianne.

"I believe I do," he said at last.

She exhaled shakily. For a moment, she'd thought all was lost.

The king rounded the tables of watching villagers and came to stand before her. He held out his hands.

"Daughter, I have wronged you, and I'm sorry for it. Will you forgive me?"

The room held its breath.

"Of course," Brianne said, clasping his outstretched palms.

The villagers cheered, and Colleen and Eva shouted the loudest of all. Declan hugged her close, and the king nodded.

"Now," he said, "will you *please* serve me some of this delicious meal everyone has been praising?"

The celebration went well into the night. After the feasting, they pushed the tables back against the walls and there was music and dancing and revelry until everyone got hungry again. They ate, and then the children were put to bed under the tables while the dancing started up again, followed by toasts and tales until dawn was near.

Despite her father's pleas for Brianne and her husband to come live at the castle, she declined.

"Who would help the miller and his wife, if we left?" she asked.

"But we miss your cooking," Eva said, lacing her arm through Brianne's.

"Then you'll have to come visit, and I'll make you dinner." Brianne frowned, "Although the miller's house is a bit small."

"Then let a new one be built beside the mill, at my expense," the king said. "With a large dining room."

"And a larger kitchen," Colleen said, laughing. "Oh, Bri, I'm so glad for you. No matter what Eva says, we missed more than your cooking."

"Then, once the new house is built, you'll have to come for supper once a week," Brianne said.

"That we will," the king declared, and the matter was settled.

As dawn filled the sky, Brianne and Declan went home,

hand in hand. Rose and gold painted the clouds overhead, but nothing could match the glow of contentment in her heart. At last, she had everything she'd ever wanted: her family, her true love, and the promise of a kitchen of her own. She would stock it with all the finest herbs and spice.

And, of course, plenty of salt.

~*~

THE WITCH OF THE WOODS

CHAPTER 1

WINTER FELL HARD over the land of Steenbeck, bringing fierce blizzards that howled louder than starving wolves at the door. Thick snow and icy frosts drove the animals deep into their dens, and withered every growing thing until even the trees of the dense forests were shriveled and dry. The people in the city felt hunger's pinch, those in the villages curled up around aching bellies at night, but the worst off, by far, were those living in the isolated cottages of farm and forest.

Among those who ate handfuls of snow to try to fill their stomachs, who felt their limbs shake with weakness as they set snares that remained empty, were the household of the woodcutter, Bergen.

Bergen had two children. Hayden, a tall lad old enough to be out on his own, and a younger daughter, Graciele, a clever girl, who had never known her mother. Though Bergen's wife had died in childbirth, the children had inherited their mother's coloring: dark brown hair, strong jawlines, and striking eyes the color of a clear green river, shading to dark amber in the center.

After his first wife passed, Bergen thought he might wed again, to provide a new mother for his children. Unfortunately, he chose poorly.

The new stepmother was a greedy woman who had married the woodcutter based upon the gossip that he possessed a secret store of silver. His first wife had come from a well-off merchant family, though after her death they moved away, cutting off contact with the woodcutter and his children. Surely, though, there were hidden riches in Bergen's cottage.

When the new wife discovered that the only things of value he possessed were a silver platter, a necklace set with bright rubies, and four gold-chased crystal goblets, she became bitter and unkind. Especially as the woodcutter steadfastly refused to hand over the jewelry, claiming he was keeping the necklace to give his daughter when she came of age.

The only thing the stepmother brought to the marriage was her pet turkey, Tom: a bird as ill-tempered as his owner. The turkey lived in a pen next to the house, and was always fed the best scraps. When the winter storms blew, he was brought inside and fed acorns, snapping at anyone who came too near.

The stepmother took her own temper out upon the children, though Hayden shielded his little sister from the woman's wrath. Five years separated him from Gracie—enough that he was soon too big for the stepmother's raised fist, and able to look after his sister when they went foraging in the woods.

"You should leave," Gracie told her brother when he reached his fourteenth birthday. Though only nine, she was wise beyond her years. "Make a better life for yourself in the city."

"I won't leave you," he said. He shivered to think what harm might befall her if she were left to face their stepmother alone.

Every spring, Gracie told him to go, and every spring, he refused.

"Once you turn sixteen," he told her, upon his own sixteenth birthday, "then we will go together to the city and find work."

"I can go now," she told him staunchly, her eleven-year-old hands closed into stubborn fists. "I'll work at the weaving mills."

Hayden shook his head. He'd heard the tales of children worked to death in the factories, and refused to let his sister trade their meager existence at the cottage for an even worse fate.

Two more years eked by, their stepmother growing harder with each winter. She began to shoot him dark, pointed looks whenever he was near, despite the fact that he could bring in at least as much wood as his father. But the price of firewood had fallen of late, and Hayden had grown tall and well-muscled, with an appetite honed by his labors.

"He eats too much," she said to his father. "Send him away so he will no longer be a burden to us."

Hayden felt his father's gaze upon him and bent his head, pretending to be absorbed in the little wooden horse he was whittling beside the fire.

"I can't," the woodcutter said. "It would break Graciele's heart."

The stepmother scoffed. "He spoils her. Better for the girl to toughen up. She needs to learn to stand on her own."

For the next several days, Hayden tread carefully and ate little, despite the hunger burning in his belly. He tried not to mention how fat the turkey was, while he and Gracie grew thinner by the month. After a week had passed without his father turning him out of the cottage, Hayden knew he was safe.

For the time being.

Now, though, the winter wind whistled in around the door and windows of their humble dwelling. There were not enough blankets to keep them warm. Even the abundance of firewood was dwindling at an alarming rate, the heat quickly sucked from the heart of the wood by the frigid air.

The family slept as close to the fireplace as they dared. Hayden draped his gray woolen cloak over himself and Gracie, while their stepmother hoarded the warmest blankets for herself.

In the dead of winter, when the snow was as high as his waist and the world was muffled in white, the old year turned to the new. More bleak months stretched ahead, yet the pantry was bare. The root crops they'd stored had shriveled and frozen and crumbled away. Every day, Hayden went out in search of game, but there was nothing. Even the mice that lived in the cottage had disappeared.

One night, as the coals glowed sullenly on the hearth, Hayden heard his stepmother whispering into Bergen's ear.

"Take your children deep into the forest," she said, "and leave them there, otherwise we will starve to death."

Their father made a sleepy protest, but Hayden could hear

there was little heart in it. "What about the turkey? You said its time was coming soon."

"It is. But think how much more there will be to eat, if there's only two of us. Besides, Hayden is full grown. He'll take care of his sister."

For three nights in a row, in the small and bitter hours of the darkness, Hayden heard his stepmother whispering, her voice low and strange. Each time, his father's protests grew weaker, until, on the third morning, Bergen would not meet his son's eyes.

"Bundle up," the woodcutter said to his children, a false heartiness in his voice. "I've heard there's a house deep in the forest, where we will find food."

Gracie gave her brother a doubtful glance, but he sent her a silent look of confidence. His fingers closed around the white pebbles in his pocket, which he'd excavated from beside the frozen stream the day before.

"Hurry, now," the stepmother said, holding out Gracie's moth-eaten cloak. "The sun is up, and there's no time for breakfast. You can eat later."

Anger shook through Hayden, and he nearly confronted his stepmother. Short of throwing her out into the snow and barring the door, though, there was little he could do—and his father would never allow it. Besides, unlike his stepmother, Hayden would not stoop to murder. Carefully, he banked his temper. Rage would only burn the precious energy he needed to keep himself and Gracie alive.

He belted on his dagger, then took his hunting bow from the wall along with a quiver of arrows, daring his stepmother to protest. Her lips tightened, but she shot a look at her husband and said nothing. When their stepmother's back was turned, he saw his sister take her gathering basket, then slip a small paring knife into her pocket.

Shoulders bowed, their father silently led them out of the cottage and into the woods. They trod the usual paths at first, but as the trees clustered more closely together and the light fought to break through the tightly woven branches, Hayden began dropping his pebbles.

He knew the forest well enough, but Bergen had been a woodcutter his entire life. As the hours passed, he led his children by unknown ways, deep into the dark heart of the woods.

Though it was winter, the densely tangled evergreens overhead trapped the snow, keeping it from landing on the forest floor. Here and there, drifts of white had broken through, but the woodcutter avoided the snow, or any place where they'd leave tracks. More proof, if Hayden needed it, that their father planned to abandon them with no return. They stepped over ground covered with rotting black leaves and shattered pine needles.

But with the help of the stones, Hayden hoped they'd be able to find their way out again.

From somewhere far away, a wolf howled. Gracie stumbled and he caught her by the arm, steadying her.

"I'm afraid," she whispered in a voice too soft for their father to overhear.

"Stay strong, and don't worry." He squeezed her hand, trying to infuse her with hope. "I'll always take care of you."

She gave him a somber nod, then turned and trailed the woodcutter into the depths of the forest. Hayden's heart tightened in his chest. No matter what happened, he vowed to protect his little sister. With his own life, if necessary.

It won't come to that, he told himself. They'd escape the forest, return to the cottage and gather up their few belongings and the things their mother had left them, and then go. For good.

He should've listened to Gracie and brought her to the city last spring, despite the fact she was still four years shy of sixteen. Had he known the grim winter that awaited, he would have.

It was obvious now that their cottage was no longer home. Leaving in the dead of winter wasn't a happy thought, but the harshness of the icy road was still better than starving to death in the woods. He knew that, as long as their stepmother lived, she would never let them set foot in the cottage again.

With such dark thoughts for company, he followed his sister into the icy shadows, strewing the rocks behind them—patches of white shining like weak stars against the bitter ground.

CHAPTER 2

"We'll rest here," the woodcutter said when they reached a small clearing surrounded by hunched black evergreens. "Gather some kindling, and we'll build a fire."

Midday had shifted to afternoon, and Hayden had no idea where they were in the vastness of the forest. He only had one stone left in his pocket. If their father led them any deeper into the woods, they'd be hopelessly lost.

"Well?" The woodcutter gestured sharply. "There's plenty of sticks at hand. Go fetch them. I'll make a fire ring."

Exchanging a look, Gracie and Hayden began to scavenge for small branches. He kept an eye on his father, who'd unearthed a few rocks and was arranging them in a circle. Maybe the woodcutter had changed his mind, and wouldn't be leaving them, after all?

A few moments later, Hayden turned with his arms full of kindling, and his heart sank.

The clearing was empty, the fire ring abandoned. While their backs had been turned, Bergen had soundlessly disappeared into the shadowed depths of the forest. His woodcraft skills were unsurpassed, despite the years that had turned his once-black hair to gray.

"Father?" Gracie whispered, though her voice held an undertone of hopelessness.

Hayden dropped his wood to reach over and take her mittened hand. "He's gone."

She let out a muffled sob, and he pulled her into a hug, trying to give them both comfort.

"Don't worry," he said softly. "I have a plan."

Sniffling, his sister listened, and when he finished telling her what they were to do next, she pulled in a ragged breath.

"Back to the cottage? Do you really think our stepmother will simply let us gather our belongings and go?"

"She wishes to be rid of us. And Father won't stop us leaving."

Still holding Gracie's hand, Hayden turned and scanned the forest floor. A telltale gleam of white marked the ground beneath the trees and he went toward it. The first stone. He bent and pocketed it, then kept going, scanning the shadows for the waystones he'd left behind.

In this manner, they picked their way back through the somber trees. Sometimes it took both of them casting about for several minutes to find the next stone. Night had fallen, black and frigid, by the time they returned to more familiar trails.

"We'll be there soon," Hayden said, noting how Gracie shivered with cold.

Sometime later, he glimpsed the warm glow shining from the cottage windows. Slowly, he and Gracie approached.

"Wait," he said quietly when she headed for the door.

Instead, he led them around to the side window. He

boosted Gracie up, and they peered in through the glass. She sucked in a sharp breath, and Hayden narrowed his eyes at the sight within.

Their father and stepmother were seated at the small table, a feast spread out before them. Roast turkey, buttered potatoes, and a dish of orange carrots filled the table. Hayden's mouth watered at the sight.

"She killed Tom," Gracie whispered.

He nodded. That plump fowl upon the table could only be the pet their stepmother had cosseted for so many years. He wondered if it had shrieked when she'd butchered it. But where had the rest of the bounty come from?

Two creamy new candles shed warm light over the scene. Hayden's heart turned to ice as he watched his father guzzle his tankard of ale, then smile over at his wicked wife.

Gracie was the first to understand what had happened.

"Mama's platter is gone. And the box with the necklace." She looked at Hayden, her eyes wide in her thin face. "Even our clothes chests. Did she sell *everything* that belonged to us?"

He scanned the room, realizing his sister was right. Their mother's legacy was gone, along with anything that could not be used by his father and stepmother. Even the little collection of carved animals he'd made for Gracie over the years had disappeared. It was as if he and his sister's presence had been completely erased.

There was no point in going inside. There was nothing left in the cottage for them to claim. Hayden was grateful for the foresight that had prompted him to bring along his weapons and throw on his extra cloak.

Shoulders slumped, Gracie dropped down from the window.

"Do we make for the road now?" she asked.

Hayden shook his head. "We'll rest in the woodshed a few hours, then leave before dawn."

It wasn't much shelter, being open along the front, but it blocked the frigid wind, and huddling in the shed was better than braving the freezing road in the darkness. Besides, he'd noted that the wood box inside the cottage was piled high. Neither his father nor stepmother would venture out to gather more wood for the fire until morning.

By then, he and Gracie would be on the road to the city. A hard journey, to be sure, but they had no other choice.

They made a rough nest beside the split logs, and Hayden spread his extra cloak over them. The stars shone down, merciless and uncaring, but beautiful in their silver light. He traced the constellations and watched the small curve of the moon rise, until his eyes were heavy enough to close.

When the barest hint of pewter shone in the east, Hayden woke his sister. Silently, they stepped out of the shed and passed the dark cottage. No light shone from the windows, and only a thin trail of smoke emerged from the chimney. He left it behind without a backward glance.

Their boots crunched over the rime of ice on the road as they went through the sleeping village, barely illuminated by the lowering moon. A dog barked at them from inside a stable, and here and there they heard the muffled sounds of households awakening. Then they were past, and gradually the world around them grew more visible as night retreated.

The bare, white fields outside the village were replaced

by dark evergreens encroaching upon the road. Gracie shivered, shooting a wary look at the trees looming on either side.

"Something's watching us," she whispered, her voice edged with fear.

He set his hand to his dagger and scanned the forest. Gracie had shown a growing woodsense over the past few years, and he'd learned to listen to her. From the corner of his eye, he caught a gray shadow ghosting through the underbrush. Eyes glinted from the shadows.

"Wolves." Gracie caught his elbow.

"Keep walking. Slowly." He pulled his bow from his shoulder and nocked an arrow to the string, his nerves taut.

Then, out of the underbrush, a snarling figure lunged, fangs and fur and yellow eyes that promised doom.

"Run!" Hayden cried, even as he loosed his arrow.

The point lodged in the wolf's flank, and the creature yelped and sheared away. Heart pounding, he grabbed another arrow and set it to his bow. The wolf was gone, but a moment later a series of long, wavering cries filled the air.

"This way." Gracie grabbed his arm and tugged him into the trees on the other side of the road.

"Are you sure we should go into the woods?" He didn't release his hold on the arrow.

"They're on the road," she said. "Look."

In the graying light between the trees, Hayden saw a half-dozen wolves slip onto the packed snow, a ragged semicircle cutting off their retreat.

They'd no choice but to take to the forest. Blowing out a breath, he eased his grip on his bow, keeping it at the ready. Quickly but carefully, he and Gracie hurried through the underbrush. The back of his neck prickled, and he expected a leaping attack at any moment.

But though he caught glimpses of the wolves skulking behind them, they seem content to simply trail their prey. For the moment.

"We'll circle around," he said softly. "Get back to the road."

She nodded once, shivering.

But every time they turned in that direction, the wolves were there first, skulking between them and their chosen way. When their steps slowed, the beasts howled behind them, near enough to make his blood race. It felt as though he and Gracie were being herded deep into the forest.

They were both staggering with weariness and hunger when at last the sun began to warm the woods. The sounds of pursuit behind them dwindled, and then were gone. He turned, but the wolves at their heels had evaporated like mist. Gracie looked at him, dark smudges of weariness beneath her eyes.

"Now what?" she asked.

"We find water, and then we rest."

The hunger cramping his belly was a familiar companion, but the thirst burning through him was new. There were no snowdrifts nearby, but he spotted a thin game trail off to their left. It should eventually arrive at one of the many streams threading through the forest.

"This way," he said, leading his sister to the narrow opening in the underbrush. He kept his tone light, setting his teeth against the knowledge that they were hopelessly lost.

Their father hadn't managed to abandon them in the forest, but now they were equally lost, with no stones to guide them out. At least the bitter chill of night had faded.

He wasn't sure if it was weariness, or his imagination, but between one step and the next, Hayden's skin prickled. An emerald glow seemed to fill the air for a heartbeat, then was gone. He shot Gracie a quick look.

"Did you feel that?"

She nodded somberly. "There's magic here. Look." She reached up and gently grasped a thin alder branch. "Buds."

"It's not spring yet." He peered at the branch, seeing the first swellings of green. "Are we in any danger from it?"

She cocked her head, as if listening intently. "I don't think so. Not now, at any rate. And I don't sense the wolves at all."

Trading a mysterious enchantment for the creatures that had been hunting them seemed, at first glance, a good thing. But the deepest part of the forest held strangeness. When they were young, their father had told them stories of impossible creatures half-glimpsed through the underbrush, and the villagers whispered tales of a witch that lived deep in the forest and ate any ill-behaved children who crossed her path.

"Do you think we'll see her?" his sister asked as they continued along the game trail. "The Witch of the Woods?"

"That's just a story to frighten children into obedience. Even if there was once a witch dwelling in the forest, she's long gone by now."

Gracie made a doubtful sound; but encountering some mythical witch was the least of their worries.

Every step took them deeper into spring. Now the trees sported yellow-green leaves, the evergreens tipped with new growth. The underbrush thickened, a few pink flowers shining through the green.

The babble of running water pulled them on, and soon they reached a stream surrounded by brushy willows. Watercress carpeted the bank, and the water ran clear and lucent over brown stones. He and Gracie went to their knees and stripped off their mittens, hastily scooping the water into their cupped palms and drinking deeply.

Once his thirst was slaked, Hayden sat back on his heels and surveyed the forest. Gracie offered him a handful of cress and he chewed it slowly, savoring the peppery taste.

They needed food and shelter—something to protect them when night fell.

At least the harsh edge of winter was no longer biting at their heels. Though it was unsettling, perhaps stumbling into enchantment wasn't all bad.

CHAPTER 3

THEY SPENT the rest of the morning following the stream. Hayden glimpsed a few rabbits darting away, their sleek coats still brown, unlike the winter-white hares in the rest of the woods. There was deer scat on the trail, too, and he felt his worry ease. They would not starve here.

They were stumbling with weariness when they finally came to a tall cedar, its draping boughs providing a rough shelter. They ducked under the branches and gathered fragrant boughs to make a nest. Gracie lay down and immediately fell asleep, but he remained watchful, his thoughts restless.

"We could make camp here," he said, once she woke.

Sitting, she plucked fronds of cedar from her hair, then glanced about. "No. The forest wants us to move on."

He frowned, wanting to argue. But Gracie shared a connection with the woods. She could always find the mushrooms hiding beneath fallen leaves, and knew where the berry bushes held their last, sweet fruit.

"As long as we don't return to winter," he said, tightening

the clasp of his cloak and ducking out from under the tree. "Where to?"

Gracie followed, then turned in a slow circle.

She pointed toward the stream. "That way."

They hopped across, then he hung back, letting his sister choose their path. With a quick smile at him, she headed into the woods, picking a meandering route between the evergreens.

Afternoon sunlight broke through the trees in slanting beams, and here and there a thrush sang from the high branches. Ferns brushed against his boots, and small white flowers dotted the forest floor. It seemed a dream, and yet he could not deny it.

Winter had not touched this place.

Gradually, he became aware of the smell of flowers. It reminded him of his mother's herb garden—the one his stepmother had dug up and left to ruin, in a wild search for silver coins that didn't exist. She'd left the plants upended, roots exposed and trampled, or carelessly torn in half.

Although he and Gracie had tried to coax the garden back to life, they'd only been able to save a handful of plants. Mint and comfrey, and a straggling rosemary that had eventually died. At its height, the garden had been a refuge. Though he'd been only a young boy at the time, he remembered the smell of lavender, the taste of sage and savory on his tongue.

Slowly, another scent joined that of flowers. Inhaling deeply, he wrinkled his brow in disbelief.

Gracie glanced over her shoulder. "Do you smell it? Fresh bread."

"No one is baking in the middle of the forest. It must be an illusion." He felt dizzy with hunger.

"Maybe." His sister turned and continued through the trees.

The scent wrapped around them, luring them on. Yeast and honey, flower and fruit. Hayden was dazed by the aromas, and almost ran into Gracie when she came to a sudden halt at the edge of a clearing. At the center of the large, grassy meadow an enormous oak tree stood, towering into the clear blue sky.

Stopping beside his sister, he felt his mouth open with shock. They'd stumbled upon a garden.

But not just any garden. Instead of growing in a plot of cultivated land, fruits and flowers ascended into the oak itself. Plants spilled from boxes, they grew in the crooks of branches and hung from the boughs in cleverly constructed baskets. Climbing roses intertwined with raspberry brambles, the feathery tops of carrots sheltered beneath waving coneflowers of vibrant purple and deep orange, and hardy stalks of red chard shaded the delicate leaves of basil.

Half-hidden by the abundant foliage, he spied a narrow staircase spiraling up around the trunk of the huge oak.

"It smells so good," Gracie said, starting forward again.

Before he could stop her, she'd reached the tree and plucked a crimson raspberry from among the creamy petals of the roses. She popped it in her mouth, and a look of bliss spread over her face.

"Gracie..." he said warningly.

"I couldn't help it. I'm so hungry, and it's so delicious. Here." She plucked another berry, then popped it in his mouth when he was about to protest.

Ambrosia exploded against his tongue, and he was unable to spit the fruit out as he'd intended. His sister was right—this was one of the most amazing things he'd ever tasted. He couldn't stop himself from reaching above Gracie's head and picking a few more of the delectable berries.

"Look." She mounted the first few steps of the staircase and grabbed a ripe pear from a small fruit tree magically grafted onto oak tree's trunk.

Hunger crashed down on Hayden and he joined his sister on the stairs. Instead of taking a pear, he dug into one of the nearby boxes and pulled a pale orange carrot from the soil. He brushed off the earth clinging to it then took a bite.

It was astounding how sweet and good the simple root tasted.

Gracie moved up a few more steps. The scents twined around them, underscored by the buzzing of bees and the rustle of wind in the leaves. Were they dreaming, while their frozen bodies lay somewhere on the forest floor?

Surely this could not be real.

"Come up," his sister called. "I found a honeycomb."

If this were a dream, then he would enjoy it to the fullest.

He ascended around the curve of the tree trunk to find his sister sitting on the stairs. She had a golden piece of honeycomb in one hand and a palmful of small red tomatoes in the other. Blue morning glories twisted around the banister, and he glimpsed the hearty leaves of potato plants spreading from a crook in the branches.

Gracie held the honeycomb toward him, and he took a bite. If he'd thought the raspberry was most delicious thing he'd ever tasted, he quickly revised his opinion. This was pure sunshine upon his tongue.

Then the tree shivered. A cold breeze swirled across the back of his neck, and Hayden straightened, one hand going to his dagger. Gracie's eyes widened in alarm, and she scrambled to her feet as the sound of footsteps echoed from overhead.

Someone—or some*thing*—was coming.

He shoved his sister behind him, then drew his dagger as the steps came closer. The steady tread spiraled down the stairs, then paused just above their heads.

A cold wind fluttered the plants around them, and Gracie shot him a wide-eyed look.

"Run?" she whispered.

He shook his head. "It's too late."

Whoever lived in this tree, he and his sister had eaten of their food, and would now have to face the consequences. They'd stumbled into a fairytale, and in the way of such things, he'd no doubt there was a price to pay.

The tree shook again.

After a long, heart-pounding moment, the steps resumed. Hayden balanced on the balls of his feet, ready to lunge into an attack. Gracie's breath rasped at his shoulder as they stared upward, waiting, as the hollow footsteps grew ever closer.

CHAPTER 4

PALE LEATHER BOOTS came into view first, tightly cinched around slender ankles. The hem of a forest-green cloak brushed brown leggings covered by the edge of a tunic embroidered with leaves. A thick leather belt was cinched over the tunic, holding a finely tooled belt pouch and a wickedly sharp dagger.

The person rounded the final step, and Hayden was unsurprised to see it was a woman. Her pale hair at first made him think she was a crone, but the face beneath the white-gold crown of braids was that of a younger woman. Pale blue eyes regarded him from a finely boned face, her nose long and straight, her chin pointed and stubborn looking. She did not smile. Indeed, there was something sad in her expression, as though she was deeply sorry for their presence.

"Who are you, strangers, that eat so freely of my abode?" she asked in a cold voice.

Hayden slipped his dagger back in its sheath, then bowed, as best he could manage on the narrow stairs. "Forgive us, lady. We were lost in the forest, and hunger overcame us."

Her eyes narrowed and she leaned forward almost imperceptibly, as if preparing to rush down upon them. Squaring his shoulders, he rested his fingers on the handle of his dagger. He didn't want to fight this woman, but he would do anything to keep Gracie safe.

Her eyes flicked down to his weapon and her stance eased, though her expression remained grim. "I cannot forgive you. There is a price for your transgression."

Hayden felt his sister lean over to peer past his shoulder.

"But we have no money," she said.

The woman's gaze shifted to Gracie. "Then you must pay another way."

A warning tingled down his spine. He stared at the pale-haired figure above him. "And what might that be?"

Her lips flattened into a frown. "You are bound here as my servants, for a year and a day."

Hayden heard the darkness beneath her words. "A year and a day. What happens after that?"

The sorrow in her expression intensified, and her gaze slid away from his. "Then you will be free of me."

The words held a weight of meaning—none of it good.

Gracie set a slim hand on his shoulder. "We should leave now," she said in a quiet voice.

The woman laughed, a single hard sound. "Try, if you like. But once you pass through the barrier, you cannot get out again."

"The barrier?" he asked.

"Oh," Gracie said softly. "Where we stepped through the green glow. Don't you remember?"

He gave a single, sharp nod, regretting the moment he'd let

his sister lead the way. Now they were, apparently, trapped. Not that he'd take the woman's word for it.

"Who are you?" he demanded, though there could only be one answer.

"The Witch of the Woods." Her face grew hard and a sudden wind whipped the branches of the oak tree, tearing petals off the flowers.

"You don't... look like a witch," Gracie said hesitantly.

As quickly as it had come, the witch's expression eased. The wind subsided, and overhead a bird let out a single, low whistle. A moment later, a magpie glided down to perch on the railing next to the witch. It cocked its head, regarding them.

"Hello," Gracie said.

It responded with a squawk, taking off again in a flurry of black and white feathers.

"Who was that?" Gracie asked.

"Merro," the witch said. "My familiar. Come. I have food and drink for you, and then you may rest."

She turned and began ascending the stairs, her green cloak flaring out behind her. Hayden exchanged a look with his sister.

"I'm not sure we should follow her," he said quietly, though his stomach growled in protest. "It's dangerous to eat a witch's food."

"We already did," Gracie pointed out. "That's what got us in trouble."

"Maybe. Or maybe just entering her realm did." With a shiver of foreboding, he recalled how the wolves had driven them forward into the deep heart of the forest.

"I'm hungry, though." There was a piteous note in her voice. "Besides, she hasn't hurt us."

"Yet. Don't forget, we've been cursed to stay with her for a year and a day."

He suspected from the witch's words that some dire fate awaited at the end of that time, though he didn't say as much to Gracie. He hoped she hadn't caught that implication. Frowning, he glanced at the ground a dozen feet below. Did the bones of other unfortunate travelers enrich the soil beneath the witch's oak?

His sister stepped forward and set a hand on his arm. "It's not like we have any choice."

She pushed past him before he could stop her and headed up the stairs. Shaking his head, he followed. The staircase wound around and around the oak, and soon wonder displaced his dark thoughts.

Their life in the cottage had been a hard one, filled with endless work and little reward. But here, abundance sprang from the branches of the tree. Every few steps, he noticed a new fruit or flower or vegetable growing, all intertwined together. It reminded him again of his mother's herb garden, and a pang shot through his heart at the memory.

Most of the time he was able to banish thoughts of her. Losing Mama was a wound he'd been determined to ignore, especially when his baby sister had needed him. But sometimes, in the quiet of the forest, he closed his eyes and tried to recall her smile and the sound of her voice.

Now that Gracie was older, he'd noticed how much like their mother she was beginning to look. Had their father seen it, too? Was this why he'd been so willing to abandon them both in the forest, to remove that painful reminder of the past?

Around the next curve of the staircase, they encountered an angular wall with a round window set high overhead. A few steps later they reached a tall door, standing open to the elements. Gracie hesitated on the doorstep and Hayden caught up to her. Together, they peered into the witch's house.

It was a large, single room with windows on all sides. A colorful rag rug covered most of the pale wood floor, and a large worktable was pushed against one of the sloping walls. Opposite the table was a kitchen area, with a small hearth, counters, and shelves filled with jars of preserved food. Pots and pans hung from the low ceiling, along with bunches of dried herbs and strings of garlic and onion. His stomach growled again at the sight.

There was no sign of the pale-haired witch, but at the far end of the room he glimpsed another serpentine stairway curling into the upper branches of the tree. Taking a step back, he tipped his face up to stare into the branches spreading high overhead. Now that he knew what to look for, he could make out a series of curve-edged structures ascending into the tree.

A slight movement behind him, a displacement of air, made him whirl. The witch had materialized on the steps below. She gave him a look, one brow raised.

"I see you are curious about my home," she said.

"Since it's to be our prison for the next year and a day, yes." He wouldn't let her forget they were her unwilling guests.

"It's not my fault you so rudely plundered my garden." She glanced upward. "Above you are my workshops and storage rooms."

"And do you perch at the very top of the tree, like some kind of vulture?"

Gracie poked him in the ribs. "Don't insult her," she said quietly. "If we're truly stuck here, it would be better not to make her our enemy."

The witch's cold blue eyes bored into his. "It is not for you to judge who, or what, I am. My rooms are forbidden to you, except for this common area. You and your sister will be given your own sleeping rooms."

"How do you know she's my sister?"

She gave him a pitying glance. "The two of you look much alike, but even more than that, I can sense the shared blood beating in your veins. What names do you call yourselves?"

He was reluctant to tell her. In the old tales, names had power. But Gracie ducked under his arm and fearlessly faced the witch.

"I'm Gracie," she said. "And this is Hayden. What is your name?"

The witch's gaze flicked to his sister. "You may call me Nissa."

Nissa. He tasted the sound against his tongue. It was a name he'd never heard before. But then again, he'd never encountered any woman like this strange Witch of the Woods.

One moment she seemed full of strange power, the next, she seemed the saddest person he'd ever met. He didn't know whether to be afraid of her, or try to comfort her.

But that was a foolish notion. He shook his head at himself. If he and Gracie were to survive whatever happened in a year and a day, he couldn't afford to let down his guard.

"The soup's ready." Nissa motioned for them to go into the common room. "Unless you prefer to eat it cold?"

"Not me." Gracie glanced at him. "I'm starving."

They both were, quite literally. He turned and went inside.

Whatever the future held, he and his sister needed to put more meat on their bones and regain their strength. Once they did, he intended to test the limits of the witch's power, and cross the barrier. But for now, remaining in her strange, enchanted home was a better fate than wandering, lost and hungry, in the winter woods.

CHAPTER 5

A HANDFUL OF DAYS PASSED. Every morning, Hayden made a notch on the stick he'd collected the first day, tracking the time until a year and a day was up. Not that he planned for them to be there when it arrived. He vowed he and Gracie would escape well before that fateful day.

The birds made a racket in the branches at dawn, but he and his sister were used to rising early. Their life quickly fell into a pattern, and though the witch demanded they work, it was no worse than their duties at home.

Each morning, they found a simple breakfast awaiting in the common room of the witch's tree-cradled abode. Though she never broke her fast with them, she was always there, lingering long enough to give them curt instructions before disappearing for the day, either to her highest aerie or out into the surrounding forest.

Gracie tended the garden, and was also required to sweep out their bedroom aeries and the common room, as well as the staircase that curled around the oak's sturdy trunk.

Hayden was allowed into the forest, though the magpie

always accompanied him, its bright eyes watching his every move. He cut and gathered firewood, set a few snares for rabbits, and foraged for berries and mushrooms. Gracie was better at gathering, but the witch would not allow her to set foot far from the oak.

They both fetched water from the nearby stream, however. Nissa had led them to the banks and shown them the pool she'd created by damming a portion of the water, where they could also bathe and wash their clothing. They'd arrived with nothing but the clothes upon their backs, of course, but the first morning, they'd awoken to find shirts of finely woven linen, leggings, and for Hayden, a leather jerkin that fitted him perfectly.

On the sixth day, the witch gave him a new task.

"Tomorrow is my baking day," she said. "Fetch stones to repair the oven, and mud to seal up the cracks. And replenish the woodpile."

Hayden nodded. He'd noticed the huge oven squatting at the edge of the clearing. How could he not? It stood at least seven feet high, made of rounded stones with a cavity beneath to hold the fire. The interior of the oven was big enough to bake dozens of loaves, or roast an entire deer.

Or...

A shiver crept down his spine. Were the rumors about the witch eating people actually true?

As soon as Nissa left, he turned to his sister.

"Remember Tom Turkey?" he asked in a low voice. "Fattened up, until he finally became dinner?"

She stared back at him, eyes wide. "Do you really think she means to..."

"I don't know. But I don't intend for us to be here long enough to find out."

"How will we escape?" she asked softly.

He glanced over his shoulder to make sure the witch was really gone. "I don't have a plan yet. But I will. Until then, act like nothing's wrong."

He gave her a quick hug around the shoulders, then left her to her sweeping while he went to find rocks to repair the oven.

As he hauled stones and chinked up the cracks, his mind worked at the problem. Outside the witch's enchanted domain, it was still winter. There was no point in him and Gracie trying to escape until spring had arrived, and summer would be even better. That would give them enough time to gain their strength and gather supplies for their journey out in the world.

In the meantime, they were safe. Nissa might be a strange, awkward woman, but until their service had ended, he believed she meant them no harm. Just like Tom Turkey, he though wryly, slathering clay around a newly replaced stone. The fowl had probably thought he was a coddled pet until the moment the knife descended.

The next morning, the witch woke them at first light. She waited impatiently for them to finish their breakfast, then set Gracie to mixing dough, while Hayden was sent down to make a fire beneath the oven.

"Not too hot, at first," Nissa cautioned. "The dough needs just enough warmth to rise. Later, we'll build the fire up."

When he returned from this task, she told him to wash his hands, then thrust a stoneware bowl of dough at him to knead. Gracie, a smudge of flour on her nose, looked up from the table where she was turning more dough.

"How many loaves are we baking?" she asked.

"Thirteen," the witch said shortly.

Hayden's brows rose. "That seems a bit excessive."

Nissa turned to him, hands on her hips. "Do not judge what you do not know. It is not all for us."

"Who else, then?" he asked.

"You'll see," she said, and would tell them no more.

By midday, thirteen round loaves of bread were shaped, risen, and ready to go in the oven. Three of them, Hayden noted, were marked with symbols: a crescent moon, a stylized tree, and another sigil he couldn't identify.

At Nissa's command, he fed more wood into the fire, feeling sweat dampen his forehead as he pushed another log into the fire cavity. When the witch judged the temperature to be hot enough, she and Gracie slid the loaves inside, arrayed on four large baking sheets.

"You must keep the fire burning, just so," Nissa told him. "But first, I need to show you something."

She smoothed a few wisps of pale hair back from her face, then led them to the oak. Instead of ascending the staircase, however, she rounded the huge trunk. Lengths of ivy and morning glory trailed down, making a green curtain studded with purple-blue flowers. Hayden had thought little of it, until the witch drew the foliage aside to reveal a mystery of the forest.

A weathered stone, higher than he was tall, was embedded in the trunk. Made of mica-flecked granite, it was carved with strange runes and sigils. There was a spot hollowed out in the center, like an open mouth waiting to be fed.

"This is the Stone," the witch said.

He and Gracie exchanged a glance.

"What does it do?" his sister asked softly.

"It is the source of power," Nissa answered. "It has been here for centuries, and will remain for centuries."

He blinked at her in surprise. "Have you been here that long?"

The deep sorrow that always lurked in her expression came to the fore. "No. But there has always been a Priestess of the Stone."

Gracie opened her mouth, her eyes full of questions, but the witch turned abruptly. She dropped her arm, and the curtain of foliage fell back over the Stone, hiding it once more from sight.

"Come tend the fire," she said, striding away toward the oven.

As they followed the witch, Hayden glanced back over his shoulder. Whatever the Stone was, it had an eerie, eldritch feel, an ancient magic that cared not for the lives of humans.

Unease crept down his back. Maybe they all were Tom Turkey, Nissa included.

His fears weren't eased when, later that afternoon, the witch performed her ritual. After the bread was taken from the oven and allowed to cool, Nissa took a length of pristine white linen and, chanting all the while in some strange language, carefully wrapped the three marked loaves.

A wind stirred the clearing, swirling about the witch and teasing a strand of Gracie's hair from her braid. Nissa lifted her bundle of bread to the four directions, calling out her strange invocations, then led them in a circle around the base of the oak.

The third time they rounded the tree she halted before the hidden Stone. The witch nodded to Gracie to pull aside the hanging curtain of greenery, showing her where to hook the vines back out of the way. Eyes wide, his sister complied while Nissa unwrapped the bread. She kept the loaf with the strange sigils, but gave the moon-marked one to Gracie.

After a moment's hesitation, she turned to Hayden.

"You were not expected, yet you are here." With that cryptic pronouncement, she handed him the loaf with the roughly drawn tree. "Repeat what I do."

Gracie looked at him, but he lifted one shoulder in a shrug. He had no more idea than his sister what was going on.

Nissa began to chant again, a low singsong that rose and fell hypnotically. She raised her loaf, and, tentatively, Gracie and Hayden mimicked the motion. Then she set the bread in the empty mouth of the Stone.

A sudden flare of green fire made Hayden step back, and his sister gasped out loud as the loaf was consumed in an instant. Nothing was left behind—not even a smear of soot on the empty gray stone,

"Now you," the witch said softly, nodding to Gracie.

Biting her lip, Gracie stepped forward. She set her loaf in the niche, snatching her hands back as the green fire blazed around the bread, then was gone. When the witch's gaze went to him, Hayden made his tree-marked offering, laying his loaf in the hollow.

For a moment, nothing happened. Nissa frowned slightly, a line between her eyes.

Then green flame blazed from the Stone. With a little yelp,

Gracie leaped back, and even Nissa swayed away. Not only was the bread consumed, but the runes inscribed in the granite glowed with a stark emerald light.

The clearing was suddenly silent. No wind blew, no birds sang.

A moment later, the Stone went dark again, the strange magical glow vanishing as quickly as it had come. The witch breathed out, a slow exhalation.

"Unexpected," she said softly, her expression still troubled. "Come. This part of the ritual is done."

She unhooked the ivy and morning glory vines, letting them fall closed over the Stone, then went back to where the ten unmarked loaves sat upon the wire rack next to the oven.

"There's more ceremony?" Hayden asked, striding at her shoulder. "I'm not sure I like your magical rituals."

"You're not required to like them." Her expression eased. "But this next part is far simpler, and will go quickly, with the two of you to help."

"No more green fire?" Gracie asked.

Nissa unbent enough to give her a faint smile. "No. We simply scatter crumbs from the oak tree into the forest. One loaf each, which leaves enough bread for us to eat for the rest of the week."

She handed them each a loaf, still slightly warm from the oven. Hayden resisted the urge to rip his open and take a bite, though his belly growled at the thought.

The witch sent him a wry look. "When we're done, you can have a loaf with dinner."

Although breakfast was always waiting for them in the morning, Nissa had told them to make use of the bounty of the garden for their other meals. Gracie always prepared some kind of dish for supper, leaving a lid on the pot afterward, and in the morning the food would be gone.

"I'll make vegetable stew," Gracie said. "Too bad you didn't get to check your snares today, Hayden."

"After this, I'll go. Maybe we can add a rabbit to the pot." He glanced at Nissa. So far, she hadn't joined them for any meals, but it felt rude to outright exclude her. "Will you eat with us tonight?"

Her eyes widened, and a slight flush stained her cheeks. Their gazes held for a moment, and in her eyes he saw deep, sorrow-filled yearning.

"Ah," she said, clearly at a loss for words. Then she cleared her throat. "Yes. I will."

The magpie swooped over the clearing, having been conspicuously absent during the Stone ritual. It let out a trilling cry, black and white wings flashing. Nissa glanced up at it and nodded, then shook herself, as if recalling her duties.

"Come," she said, tearing off a piece of bread as she headed for the oak.

This time, there was no chanting, no eerie fire. Hayden and his sister followed the witch in a spiraling path out from the base of the oak. He saw Gracie shoot the vine-hidden Stone a wary look each time they passed, until they reached the sunlit margins of the clearing.

They went a short distance into the woods, until they each ran out of bread. Hayden dusted off his hands.

"I'll go check my snares now," he said. "See you at dinner."

Nissa nodded gravely, but Gracie grinned at him, her good spirits restored.

"Don't take too long," his sister said. "Or I might eat all the bread before you get back."

He shot her a look and, shaking his head, strode off into the woods.

CHAPTER 6

As the lowering sun bathed the oak tree in golden light, Nissa descended from her highest aerie to the common room where Hayden and his sister waited. She was quiet and pale as she entered, her eyes shadowed with the trace of sadness that never left her expression. The table was set for three, the loaf of bread in the center surrounded by a large pat of butter, a pot of honey, and a dish of raspberry jam.

"There you are," Gracie said, stirring the pot set on the hearth. "Everything's ready. Here."

She ladled out a bowl of rabbit stew and handed it to Nissa. The witch stood uncertainly for a moment, and Hayden pulled out a one of the chairs around the table for her.

"My lady," he said, gesturing her to sit.

Again, that faint flush touched her cheeks. She didn't meet his eyes as she took her seat.

"Hayden, bring the water pitcher," Gracie said, setting their bowls on the table.

She scooted around to the long bench on the opposite side,

leaving the other chair for him, and offered the witch a piece of bread.

It was strange, treating Nissa like a guest in her own home. But she had never once, in the week since they'd arrived, eaten a meal with them in the common room. Indeed, Hayden had wondered if she was human at all, or whether she took her sustenance from the air and sunshine, like the plants did.

Now, though, as Hayden poured water into three cups made of bark, she took a bite of bread. He settled himself in the chair next to her and helped himself to two slices of the loaf.

"I'm hungry," he said when Gracie shot him a look.

Indeed, he made short work of the first piece, the long-awaited reward for their day of labor. It tasted delicious. The creatures of the forest seemed to think so, too, for when he'd returned from checking his snares, a plump rabbit slung over his shoulder, all the breadcrumbs they'd scattered had been gone.

"This is excellent," Nissa said, after her first bite of stew. "Thank you."

"You're welcome to take any of your meals with us." Gracie gave her an encouraging smile, though Hayden wasn't quite as enthusiastic about the witch's presence. They were still trapped there, after all.

As they ate, an uncomfortable silence fell, broken only by the soft sound of birds settling in for the night.

"Do you like to play games?" Gracie asked abruptly, obviously casting about for something to break the tension.

"Games?" Nissa blinked at her as though she'd never heard the word before.

"You know..." Gracie whirled her spoon in the air. "Amusements to pass the time."

Hayden leaned back and folded his arms, curious to see how this conversation would go. It had been a long time since he and his sister had sat before the fire in the cottage, rolling wooden dice or playing with the faded deck of cards.

Their laughter had displeased their stepmother, and she'd taken the cards and dice away.

"Idle hands have no place in this house," she'd said, thrusting a pile of clothing at Gracie. "These need mending. And you, Hayden, sort through this bag of beans and take out any rocks you find."

That put an end to their games, though sometimes in the long summer twilights they'd linger outside, taking turns throwing stones at a makeshift target, or telling one another tall tales, each one more ridiculous than the last.

"I have no need for amusements," the witch said somberly.

Gracie frowned, and Hayden unfolded his arms.

"Everyone needs a little fun," he said. "I don't suppose you have a deck of cards?"

Nissa looked at him as though he'd asked if she had a mountain of rubies or a pet dragon. "No."

"I'll whittle a pair of dice, then," he said. "We can start with that."

"If you insist." Her tone was dry.

"We can bet with acorns," Gracie said. "And if you make a checkers board, Hayden, I'll collect the pieces. There are some crabapple that will do, for starters."

The witch looked reluctant, but she made no protest. As soon as the meal was ended, however, she took her leave and disappeared silently up the stairs.

"I don't understand her," Hayden said, after she was gone.

"She's a witch," Gracie said. "I don't know if we can. But she seems so sad. Maybe our games will cheer her up."

"Maybe." He was more interested in amusing himself and his sister, honestly. But if Nissa joined in, he supposed he wouldn't mind.

It was true that a deep melancholy clung to her, like an invisible cape of mist and shadows. He wondered what it would take to lift it, and who she might be beneath that cloak of sorrow.

He shook the thought away. Whether or not the Witch of the Woods was unhappy was no business of his. As long as she didn't inflict her misery on them.

True to his word, Hayden carved a set of dice, and he and Gracie taught the witch a few simple games. At first she played stiffly, as though unsure whether she might enjoy herself, but after a winning streak that left Gracie laughing in despair, Nissa finally smiled.

"I won," she said, scooping all the acorns to her side of the table. "I won the game."

"You did." Hayden couldn't help a small grin. Who would've thought he and Gracie would end up playing dice with the Witch of the Woods?

As the weeks went by, they expanded to checkers and stone-drops, and once or twice Nissa even laughed. She always caught herself immediately, however, schooling her expression back to its usual reserve.

Gracie, however, grew downright cheerful. It lightened his

heart to see her regain the happy disposition she'd had as a young girl, before the harshness of life in the cottage had stolen her smiles.

For that alone, he was grateful to the witch. Despite the fact they were trapped in a bargain with her that he suspected would only end in doom.

CHAPTER 7

THREE MONTHS PASSED, by Hayden's reckoning. By now, spring would be returning to the outside world—though it was hard to believe that the seasons even existed, caught as they were in the eternal summer of the witch's domain.

It was not a terrible life. Indeed, though he didn't like to admit it, they were both thriving. No longer a half-starved waif, Gracie's hollow cheeks and bony wrists had filled out, and he was finally getting enough to eat, his muscles strong and well-defined after weeks spent chopping wood, hauling water, and making various repairs to the tree-cradled rooms.

Still, he could never quite banish the thought of Tom Turkey being fattened for the pot.

Nissa was teaching Gracie herbcraft, which she took to instantly, and how to tend the garden. And, to Hayden's dismay, the witch was also giving her increasingly larger parts to play in the weekly ritual of the Stone. It had started with Nissa showing his sister how to mark the loaves, and then how to wrap them precisely in the cloth.

The next time they performed the ceremony, he was

appalled to hear Gracie lifting her voice and joining Nissa in her chanting.

Pulse pounding, he rounded on the witch. "What are you doing? My sister isn't part of your magic."

Nissa's eyes darkened. "Since she is here, she is part of it. You both are."

"That doesn't mean you should teach her the words and gestures!"

She let out a low breath, nostrils flaring. "It does."

He reached to take her by the shoulders, to demand she stop teaching Gracie immediately, but she ducked out from under his grasp.

"Do not interrupt the ceremony," she said, an undercurrent of power in her voice.

"Hayden, stop it," Gracie added. "I like learning about the Stone."

"Without it, we would not have this." Nissa waved her arm, encompassing the clearing and the majestic oak tree. "It brings us the bounty of summer. And it must be fed accordingly. We all benefit from the magic here."

The two of them turned back to the ritual, leaving him staring darkly at the Stone. It seemed to him that the green fire held a flickering menace, a buried malice that threatened them all.

That evening, he had little appetite. The single piece of bread he ate lay like a rock in his belly, and he excused himself early to go up to his aerie.

Not long after, Gracie followed him. She sat in the open doorway, dangling one leg into the air without fear of the high drop beneath. Evening light touched the green leaves and gilded a lock of her dark hair as she glanced over at him.

"It's nothing to worry about," she said reassuringly. "Nissa just wants us to feel included."

"It's everything to worry about," he replied, leaning against the wall with his arms folded. "We don't belong here. In fact, it's high time we thought of leaving."

"Stop towering over me, and sit down," she said.

Reluctantly, he uncrossed his arms. "She's not our friend," he said sternly.

"I know." She swung her leg back and forth. "But she's not our enemy either. She's never led us into the forest and left us, or sold our mother's things." Her voice dipped at the end, and he dropped down to settle beside her, their shoulders touching.

"I suppose she's been kind enough, in her own way," he said softly. "But we can't stay. There's a city out there waiting for us."

She shot him a look. "What if I don't want to go to the city?"

"Gracie." He couldn't help his exasperation. "At the end of the year and a day, something bad's going to happen. We need to be gone before then. Summer's coming, and that's the best time for us to leave."

She pressed her lips together in a little scowl, then abruptly changed the subject.

"Your birthday is in three days."

"It is?" Now it was his turn to frown. "How do you know?"

"I'm not the only one keeping track of time, silly. I'll ask Nissa if I can make a honeycake to celebrate." She let out a sigh. "You'll be a man."

"I'm already a man," he pointed out.

She pulled up her legs and wrapped her arms around her

knees. Outside, the sun was setting, the robins making sleepy chirps as they settled for the night.

"You'll be official, though," she said. "All grown up."

"If we leave soon, we can celebrate your birthday in the city." If they were lucky. "I'll buy you a scarf with flowers embroidered on it."

She gave him a smile, though there was something sad about the edges.

He got to his feet. "Off to bed with you, and don't worry about me."

"Goodnight." She rose and kissed him on the cheek, then went down the curve of stairs to her room, leaving Hayden alone with his brooding thoughts.

His first task would be creating a stash of food. Dried fruit, hard biscuits, nuts—supplies they could travel with until they reached more inhabited lands. In a week or so, he figured he'd have enough stored up that they could leave.

They had to escape, before Gracie was pulled any further into the witch's web.

The next morning he rose early, ate a hasty breakfast, and was stepping out of the common room as his sister arrived. There was no sign of Nissa, and he was glad not to see the pale-haired witch lurking about.

"I'm going out to forage," he told Gracie. "I'll see you at supper."

"Don't forget," she called as he headed down the stairs, "I'm baking you a cake."

He waved one hand over his head in acknowledgement,

then paused to pluck a few ripe raspberries and fill his pockets with hazelnuts and a pear for lunch. His mind whirled with plans for their escape. Over the last few weeks, he'd been scouting around the forest, and today he'd explore even deeper.

The magpie accompanied him, and though the bird's steady regard made him uncomfortable, he'd begun talking to it. Partially for the company, for he could admit he was lonely, and partially to keep it from becoming suspicious as he rambled further from the witch's clearing. As he strode out, it flew over his head, black and white wings flashing, and landed on a nearby branch.

"Looking for mushrooms, today," he told it, hoisting the carrying bag he'd brought.

He went to the stream, skirted the bathing pool, then headed down the game trail that, so far, had proved promising. It meandered around thickets and over fallen logs, away from the clearing. But would it take them far enough away?

Nissa would come after them—he'd no doubt of that. But he sensed she was tethered there, to her strange house built among the branches. As long as he and Gracie fled far and fast, he thought the witch wouldn't be able to follow them beyond her enchanted domain.

She might send her magic after them, but other than the Stone rituals, he hadn't seen much evidence of her powers.

At midday the path obliged him by passing through a small clearing where bolete mushrooms grew, yellow-pored beneath a cap of slippery brown. He filled his sack, then sent a glance under the spreading alder trees where the game trail continued.

The magpie let out a squawk, and he glanced up at it. No point in rousing its suspicions further.

"You're right. The day's getting on, and there's a cake waiting for us." With a silent sigh, he turned and headed back toward the witch's house.

His mood had improved, now that he'd made up his mind it was time to leave. At dinner, he managed not to frown at Nissa, though he reserved most of his conversation for his sister. The cake was delicious, and after supper Gracie presented him with a bracelet she'd made out of braided yarrow stalks.

"It's nice," he said, fastening it around his wrist, though the stems poked his skin.

"We match." Gracie held up her arm, showing him the bracelet adorning her own plump forearm.

Hayden glanced at her round, rosy cheeks, recalling she'd taken two slices of the cake. Slowly, he pushed away his own second slice, half-eaten. They were both growing a bit too well-fed, and he recalled once again the fate of Tom the turkey.

"Don't you like my cake?" Gracie asked, glancing at his plate.

"Very much. I'm saving the rest for breakfast." He managed to smile at her. "Thank you."

"Here." Nissa reached into her pocket, then held out her hand, fingers closed. "I have a gift for you, as well."

He stared at her a moment, wishing he could refuse. He wanted no part of the witch, or her so-called gifts. It was only Gracie's beseeching expression that made him slowly reach out his hand.

Nissa held her hand over his palm, and for a moment their

fingers brushed. The contact tingled through him, making his senses flare. Their gazes caught, held, and he glimpsed something yearning in her eyes. Then she abruptly looked down and set something in his hand.

He'd been bracing himself for something unpleasant; a venomous spider, perhaps, or a sharpened thorn. Instead, he blinked down at a rounded hunk of amber, rich and golden-red, still warm from her touch. He held it up, seeing dapples of brighter gold inside.

"It reminded me of your eyes," she said, a flush coloring her cheeks.

"Thank you," he said, sincerely.

It was a rich gift. But it still couldn't make up for the fact they were trapped there, being fattened up for some unknown fate.

CHAPTER 8

LITTLE BY LITTLE, Hayden added to the cache of food he'd hidden. When he judged it was enough to sustain him and Gracie for several days' journey, he smuggled the sack of food, plus their winter cloaks, to a hiding place out beyond the stream. He'd risen at dawn, and had been able to avoid the magpie's notice both coming and going.

"Tomorrow," he said softly as he and his sister made their way up the twisting staircase to their respective bedrooms that evening. "Slip away from your chores in the midmorning. I'll meet you by the alder tree at the edge of the clearing."

Gracie glanced at him, but despite the doubt in her expression, she made no argument.

The wind blew restlessly that night, making his aerie sway back and forth, sneaking through the chinks in the walls and tugging his hair across his face.

After tossing and turning for far too long, he rose and went to sit in the small window seat carved into the opposite wall. He settled cross-legged and listened to the sound of the breeze creaking in the branches, the leaves whipping back and forth. It was almost as if the tree sensed that he and Gracie were planning to go.

Now that they were on the verge of leaving, he could admit he'd miss the enchanted clearing and magically bounteous tree. He might even miss the witch, and the glimpse of something unattainable he'd seen in her eyes.

But he wouldn't miss the Stone and its frightening, mysterious power.

With a deep breath, he made himself go back to bed, though sleep was long in finding him.

The bright calling of birds broke his hard-won slumber, and he opened his eyes to see dappled sunlight warming the floor. He lay quietly for a moment, going through plans in his head, then rose and dressed himself in the clothing Nissa had provided. Fine linen shirt, leather trousers and tunic, and woolen cloak. For the first time, he wondered if they had been crafted with magic, and if they would fall to tattered leaves and cobwebs the moment he stepped beyond her realm.

He picked up the hunk of amber, considering, then set it back down on the windowsill. Though it was worth gold, it was entirely possible the witch could track his presence using it. He and Gracie couldn't take any chances.

As usual, breakfast was laid upon the table. His sister was already there, eating a piece of bread slathered with raspberry jam. She gave him a guarded look, her gaze sliding to where Nissa stood, arms crossed, looking out one of the high windows.

"Good morning," Hayden said, reaching for a wedge of creamy cheese and a handful of nuts.

The hazelnuts went in his pocket, but he polished off the cheese and a crisp green apple. Gracie cleared their dishes, and then the witch turned, pale braids swinging across her back as she pivoted. Her piercing blue eyes made Hayden feel as though she could sense every thought in his head. It took all his discipline to meet her gaze and hold it. A shadow moved over her expression, and she was the first to look away.

"I'll draw water today, then gather more firewood," he said steadily. "Unless you have different work in mind?"

"No." Nissa's voice was low. She looked at Gracie. "Your task this day is to sweep the stairs from top to bottom, then gather the fallen nuts and fruits dislodged by the wind."

Gracie nodded, and the witch drew her cloak more tightly about her shoulders and strode out the door without a word of farewell. Though that wasn't unusual a strange heaviness lingered in the air, as if something important had been left unsaid.

"I suppose we'd best get to work," he said to his sister, with a good humor he didn't quite feel.

"I'll see you later, then," she said somberly.

He fixed her with a significant look, and she dipped her head in acknowledgement before they each went their separate ways.

The air was warm as Hayden descended the twisting staircase, carrying the stout water bucket. There was a stoneware cistern in the kitchen that held about four bucket's worth of water, and he'd noticed it was running low.

Black and white, the magpie came to settle on a low branch of a nearby evergreen. It cocked its head, regarding him with one bright eye.

"Getting some water," he told it as headed toward the stream.

Usually, when he stayed close to the clearing, the magpie went off on its own business. He hoped it would do so that day, especially if it looked like he wasn't going to set off into the woods.

As he fetched water, he saw Gracie sweeping the upper stairs, her dark hair tucked beneath a blue kerchief. Their paths didn't cross, and after he was done filling the cistern, he went to gather kindling. It was easy to stay close to the clearing, as the wind had brought down a number of sticks and branches.

To his relief, after watching him collect and stack firewood for a time, the magpie gave a chirp and flew away.

Gracie's sweeping finally took her to the bottom of the stairs. She propped her broom on the railing and began to gather the fruit and acorns scattered beneath the tree, tucking them in the sturdy sack the witch had given her. The extra food would be useful, and Hayden was glad to see that she'd mostly filled her sack by the time she approached him.

"Water?" he asked, offering her his water skin.

She took it, then whispered, "Is it time?"

He made a show of checking the woodpile, then stretched his back, turning this way and that. There was no sign of the witch. Or the magpie.

"Yes." He took the sack from Gracie and nodded toward the forest. "Follow me."

Quickly, they strode into the shadows beneath the trees. Hayden led them to the cache, where he added the apples and acorns to their other food, making sure to keep the heaviest load for himself. He handed Gracie her cloak, slung his own across one shoulder, and then they struck out into the woods.

Once or twice, he thought he heard the sound of feathered

wings overhead, but every time he whirled and peered up into the branches, he saw nothing. With every step they took away from the witch's dwelling, he felt his spirits lighten and hope kindle in his chest.

He glanced at Gracie, surprised to see a hint of sorrow in her expression.

"What's wrong?" he asked.

"I just..." she frowned. "We didn't say goodbye."

Exasperated, he shook his head. "You don't say goodbye when you're trying to escape, Gracie."

"I know, but I'm going to miss her."

For a moment, Hayden could see Nissa clearly in his mind. Her sharp features and pale hair, the intensity of her gaze, yet the way her mouth had softened into infrequent smiles during their evenings spent telling tales and playing games.

Most of the time she was cold and self-possessed, wrapped in the armor of her magic and solitude. But sometimes that façade would melt and he'd catch a glimpse of the woman beneath, filled with a desperate sorrow and loneliness.

Unlike Gracie, he wouldn't miss her—at least not much. But he would never forget her, either.

Morning pivoted to noon, and the air grew colder. Around them, the leaves on the alder branches retreated back into the tight buds of springtime, and the path beneath their feet turned from green grasses to mud. Ahead, he glimpsed the green shine of the barrier they'd crossed to enter the witch's domain.

Smiling, Hayden turned to tell his sister they were almost out.

Then, between one step and the next, a great whirling wind set the trees around them to swaying. The air grew dark as a black cloud covered the sun. Overhead came a cacophony of screeching and cawing, as if a thousand ravens were descending.

Between one heartbeat and the next, Nissa stood before them. Gracie let out a gasp, and Hayden fell back a step, one hand on his dagger.

"Did you think to leave me so soon?" The witch's looked from him to his sister, something dark and sorrowful in her eyes.

"Yes," Hayden said. There was no use denying it.

Her expression hardened. "A year and a day has not yet passed. You cannot go."

CHAPTER 9

"You can't stop us." Though he didn't want to hurt her, Hayden drew his dagger. "Let us pass."

Nissa slowly shook her head. "I don't want to fight you."

"Then stand aside."

"I cannot." Her voice caught.

"Well, then. You give me no choice."

He slowly set down the bag of food he was carrying, then loosened his cloak and let it fall to the ground. Behind him, Gracie let out a sound of protest.

"There is always a choice." The witch stared at him, her gaze compelling. "You can return willingly."

He felt a grim smile settle on his lips. "I don't think so."

Taking advantage of the moment, he rushed forward. He'd planned to shoulder Nissa to the ground, tie her up and bundle her in her cloak, then leave her behind while he and Gracie continued their escape. He'd no doubt the witch would be able to free herself; he just wanted to slow her down enough to keep her from pursuit.

But to his surprise, Nissa whirled nimbly away from his

attack. Using his momentum against him, she swept her leg out in a move designed to bring him down. He stumbled, but managed to keep his feet. Pivoting, he caught her arm. She grabbed his wrist, and for a moment they stood, face to face. The smell of roses and raspberries ticked his senses. Then she twisted away, breaking his grip, and moved back a pace.

"Not as simple as you thought," she said tightly.

"Witch and warrior, both." He shook his head, watching her warily.

He wouldn't be able to defeat her with brute force, clearly. But it was still two against one. If Gracie could provide a distraction, he'd rush Nissa again, and this time he'd be prepared for her quick reactions.

"Be careful," Gracie said.

He flicked his gaze to her, trying to provide reassurance, but, oddly, his limbs felt strangely heavy, his mind slow. With effort, he looked back at the witch. Nissa had her hands upraised and was sketching glowing sigils in the air.

"What are you doing?" he mumbled, his tongue thick behind his teeth.

"Binding you," she said.

Grab her, he tried to shout to his sister, but all that came out was a strangled *ngh*.

Still, Gracie caught his intent. She stepped forward, and Nissa whirled, her hands aglow.

"Stay back," she warned. "I can easily enchant both of you, but the after-effects of this spell aren't pleasant. Spare yourself the pain."

Hayden tried to frown, though his lips felt frozen to his face.

"Will he be all right?" Gracie shot him a worried look.

"Yes, though he won't be able to do much for the next several days, while he recovers. Now, do I have your word that you'll come willingly?" A blue spark shot from her fingertip and hovered, sizzling, in the air.

Gracie nodded. "Yes. I'll return with you."

"Good." The witch swept her hands through the air, erasing the spark. "Then we shall go."

She turned and headed back the way they'd come. Hayden tried to resist, but his body moved after hers, his feet not under his command. When he passed the bag of supplies he'd dropped, he couldn't even bend and pick it up, though his fingers twitched with the effort.

Gracie caught the motion and scooped up the food as she followed him, bringing up the rear of their sorry procession.

By the time the oak tree came in sight, Hayden's head was pounding fiercely and his limbs were filled with a painful prickling. As he stepped stiffly into the clearing, Nissa spoke a single word, and the compulsion over him lifted.

He swayed, exhaustion hammering down, and Gracie grabbed his elbow to steady him.

"Help your brother to his room," Nissa said quietly. "And do not think to escape again. Neither I nor the Stone will allow it."

It took the better part of three weeks for Hayden to regain control over his body. There was nothing worse than carrying something only to have it drop from suddenly nerveless fingers. Once, he missed a step coming out of his room, and tumbled inelegantly several feet down the staircase until he could catch himself on the vine-wound banister.

Nissa had ceased taking her suppers with them, but shortly after they'd returned, she warned them that the barrier in the woods had moved closer.

"It will paralyze you, if you try to cross it," she said, a quiet weariness in her voice. "I'd hoped I could trust you, but you've proven otherwise."

"You can trust me," Gracie said softly, and Hayden shot her a narrow-eyed look.

No, we can't, he'd thought at her, shaking his head slightly.

His sister ignored him.

"I'll make sure Hayden behaves," she continued.

Nissa sent him a quick look, and he tamped down the impulse to apologize. He had nothing to be sorry for. If anything, she should be the one to apologize for robbing him and Gracie of their freedom.

A year and a day. The end was growing closer by the month.

He didn't know exactly when, or how, he and his sister would escape—but he vowed that somehow they would break free of the witch's domain.

CHAPTER 10

BY THE END OF SUMMER, marked on his trusty calendar stick, Hayden had fully recovered. He hauled water, chopped wood, and worked on the huge freestanding oven. There were spots all over the exterior where the clay had flaked away and smaller stones had fallen out, leaving holes where the heat could escape. Making the repairs was slow, backbreaking work—especially when he got to the top, where several of the larger stones had shifted.

He spent a number of unpleasantly warm afternoons atop the structure, bracing stones and plastering the cracks. Finally, he set the last stone and gratefully clambered down, wiping the sweat from his face.

High time for a visit to the bathing pool. He'd been thinking longingly of the cool grotto as the sun beat down on his back and the stones pinched his fingers.

Dapples of light glinted on the surface of the water, and ferns nodded softly at the pool's edge. He quickly stripped off his clothing and waded into the cool, welcoming water. Holding his breath, he dunked himself under and sat for a moment on the rounded pebbles at the bottom. Curious minnows swirled about his arms, then darted away when he wiggled his fingers at them.

Finally, when his lungs were begging for air, Hayden stood, the water cascading off his sun-browned torso. He scooped his wet hair back from his face, absently noting it was time to ask his sister for a haircut. The warm air draped itself about his shoulders, and he sighed, filled with a sudden sense of wistfulness.

Movement behind the screening bracken caught his eye, and he tensed. There was nothing dangerous within the witch's enclosure—at least he didn't think so—but still, no man likes to be caught naked and unawares.

The underbrush rustled. Something larger than a rabbit stirred behind the ferns.

"Who's there?" he called, though he had his suspicions. "Show yourself."

Slowly, Nissa emerged from the greenery. Her pale hair caught the light, and she regarded him steadily from her ice-blue eyes, something almost hungry in her gaze.

He brought his hands to cover himself and sank down in the water, though it provided little cover. "Are you spying on me?"

One of her pale brows rose. "No. Merely checking on you."

Heat flared through him, a combination of embarrassment and interest. He had, admittedly, thought of Nissa from time to time in the dark hours of the night. But considering the witch in his dreams and facing her in the nude were two different things entirely.

Her eyes flicked down his body, and a flush rose on her cheeks, as if she regretted her intrusion.

"Enjoy your bath," she said shortly, then turned and moved away, barely rustling the underbrush as she left.

He stared into the shadows of the forest for a long moment, waiting to rise until he was sure she'd really gone. Why had she been spying on him? Checking to see if he was fattening up, or was there something more behind her unexpected visit?

The water suddenly too cold for his liking, Hayden clambered out of the pool and hastily dressed himself, his clothing sticking to his damp skin.

Time was passing too quickly. If he and Gracie were to escape, he shouldn't be loitering about in forest pools. Beyond the enchanted woods, fall was arriving, with bleak winter at its heels. Soon, travel in the outside world would become treacherous. It was time he started planning again.

The next day, when he went to check his snare lines, Hayden discovered the barrier had shifted position. Instead of being located far from the witch's clearing, he glimpsed its glow in the forest behind his traps. Cautiously, he went to look at it. The green light hummed and sparkled, and his skin prickled uncomfortably when he got too close. Uneasily, he backed away.

All his snares were empty, no doubt because of the magic's proximity. Frowning, he dismantled them and reset them some distance from the enchanted boundary. Then he went to find the witch.

"The barrier has moved," he said, after he'd climbed the winding staircase to one of her upper rooms.

She moved around the table where she'd been sorting herbs and frowned at him. "I told you not to come up here."

"It seemed important. Why has the barrier come closer?"

She let out a quiet breath, her gaze skidding from him to the doorway beyond. "The enclosing has begun."

She was maddening. "Why won't you tell us anything?"

"I can tell you this much." Her eyes returned to him. "Everything has a cycle. It is time for the Stone to be renewed."

That sounded ominous. "Does this renewal include some sort of human sacrifice?"

Her expression closed. "I will speak no more of this. Now, go." She lifted one hand, blue fire flickering around her fingers.

Her non-answer told him enough. He stared at her a moment, his eyes narrowed, then turned and stalked down the stairs, frustration simmering in his belly.

Every day, the barrier came closer. Hayden began stalking its circumference, looking for any weak spots. The forest behind the emerald glow wavered, as though he were looking at it through water. The magpie accompanied him, and he didn't bother hiding what he was doing. The bird could report to the witch, if it liked, but nothing would stop him looking for a way out.

At first it took him four afternoons to complete a circuit of the magical barrier. A few weeks later, it took only two. Then one, the green glow faintly visible at night from the window of his bedroom aerie. The magic was tightening around the witch's clearing like a snare around a trapped rabbit.

Several times, he nearly made a run at the barrier, impatience burning through him, but each time, something held him back. Still, as the days passed, he felt his anxiety mounting. He and Gracie had to escape. They must find a way!

Finally, with only three days remaining until the year and a day was up, he discovered a thin place in the magical boundary. The green light passed through a gnarled rowan tree, and it seemed to him the glow was fainter around the tree. Heart pounding, he stepped closer and leaned forward, peering at the barrier, Yes. The view of the forest beyond was clearer, less wavering.

With a deep breath, he reached out and touched the emerald glimmer.

A slight prickle met his fingertips, nothing more. If he could press through safely…

The first time he and Gracie had crossed the barrier, it had let them through easily. From what the witch had said, it was only set to stop them from leaving. Once he got through, he should be able to easily step back across, fetch his sister, and escape.

He'd hidden another cache of food in his room, and their cloaks, too, as leaving now meant going into the teeth of winter. At least they were strong and well fed.

And it was still better to brave the bitter snow than end up as a human sacrifice for that thrice-cursed Stone.

Pulse pounding, he shoved his hand into the scintillating green light. His fingers tingled as though they were asleep. A moment later he pulled his hand back out and inspected it. The skin was slightly reddened, the numbness he'd felt already fading.

It might be uncomfortable, but nothing he couldn't endure. Squaring his shoulders, he stepped into the glow.

The prickle became a burn as he forced himself forward,

the barrier resisting his passage. He clenched his teeth, his vision blurring. He could do this. He must, for him and for Gracie. Keep. Going.

Pain buzzed through him, and then, like dry grass catching fire, roared up. He was falling into a pit lined with deadly sharp blades, he was falling into the sun, he was falling... into blackness.

CHAPTER 11

"...BE ALL RIGHT?" Gracie's voice, high and worried.

A quieter response from the witch, too low to catch.

"But when?" His sister sounded as though she'd been crying.

Hayden smelled scorched hair, felt the dig of sticks beneath his shoulders. He was lying on the ground. He tried to open his eyes, to reassure Gracie that he was fine, that he'd only taken a bit of a knock and would be well soon.

His body wouldn't respond. His eyelids remained shut tight, his tongue immovable as a stone in his mouth. He breathed, and that was all.

Next time he rose to the surface of consciousness he was lying on a soft pallet.

"Poor, foolish man." Nissa's voice, low and sorrowful. Her cool hand upon his cheek. "We never had a chance..." Her breath caught. "At least you'll have Gracie to look after you."

There was something here he didn't understand. His fuzzy thoughts fumbled after it, but the notion had already escaped.

Hayden awoke, managing to pry open his eyes, though it felt like his eyelids were made of stone. He was surprised to see the sturdy wood beams of the common room over his head and not the curved roof of his own aerie.

Experimentally, he twitched his fingers and toes, relieved that they responded. From somewhere nearby came the clink of metal, then the sound of vegetables being chopped.

He rolled to his side, groaning, and was glad to see Gracie in the kitchen area. She whirled, eyes wide.

"Hayden!" She rushed to his side and knelt beside him. To his distress, she began to cry.

"Hush," he said hoarsely. His throat felt as though he'd swallowed a thornbush. He managed to raise his arm and pat her on the shoulder.

"I thought I'd lost you." Her voice shook. "When we brought you back from the forest, you were barely breathing. You've been unconscious for two whole days."

Two days? Fear sliced through him. Tomorrow the year and the day would be up. The witch would sacrifice him and his sister. Put to the knife, just like Tom Turkey, and despite all his efforts, they hadn't been able to get away.

He sat, though his muscles screamed at the motion.

"Where is she?" he asked from between clenched teeth.

"Here," Nissa's cool voice responded from the doorway.

He stared at her, absently noting the echo of sorrow and weariness in her features.

"Let us go," he said. "At least let Gracie go. If you have to make a sacrifice it should be me."

The witch glanced at Gracie, her mouth tightening, then her gaze returned to Hayden. "You should not have tested the barrier."

"I had to."

She gave a single nod, her eyes locked with his.

Silence descended, full of unsaid words. After a moment, Gracie rose and went to stand before the witch. With surprise, Hayden saw that his sister had grown since their arrival. She and Nissa were the same height.

"I know you can't tell us," Gracie said, her gaze fixed on the witch's face, "but is there anything you could give us that might help?"

A look of despair, as bleak as a frozen landscape, settled over Nissa's expression. She shook her head, then whirled and hurried up the stairs. If he hadn't known better, Hayden would have thought she was about to burst into tears.

"You've upset her," his sister said, going to fetch him a bowl of broth.

"I've upset *her*?" He blinked. "I'm the one who got hurt."

Gracie ladled out the soup, then returned and gently handed him the bowl. "Yes. But she didn't mean to harm you. You should've seen how carefully she tended you while you were unconscious. There's something going on here, more than meets the eye."

"What?" he asked, half-remembering Nissa's touch upon his face. He lifted the bowl of broth shakily to his lips.

"I'm not sure." Gracie settled beside him. "But we don't have much time to figure it out."

"Tomorrow the bargain is ended," he said. "She means to sacrifice us to the Stone."

She tilted her head. "Does she? Truly, Hayden. There's something here we're not seeing."

"You're too kind." He took another swallow of soup. "Do you think she's planning to shove us into the oven, bake us up like ritual loaves?"

"Stop it."

"Then what?" he demanded, despair settling in the pit of his stomach. "What is going to happen to us?"

"I don't know." Gracie looked out the door, where the silver light of evening was dimming to twilight and sleepy robins chirped in the branches. "I only hope we all survive it."

CHAPTER 12

THE MOON WAS bright that night, and Hayden couldn't sleep. He lay in his bed, feeling the branches sway around him, hearing the whisper of wind through the leaves of the witch's bower.

In the deepest hours of the night, soft footsteps approached his door. He tensed, waiting, but the steps halted just outside. Then he heard his name, whispered in a voice as soft as cobwebs. Nissa. He didn't think she'd meant him to hear.

After a moment, she turned and went away, as quietly as she'd come.

Then, somehow, dawn was upon the land. The birds sang gleefully, caring nothing for the woes of witch or mortal. Hayden turned and stretched, letting himself waken fully, even as fear crept along the edge of his bones.

Whatever happened today, he vowed to go down fighting.

Gracie met him in the common room, the dark smudges under her eyes showing she'd gotten as little sleep as he. Though neither of them had much of an appetite, they ate a sparing breakfast of fruit and bread. There was no sign of Nissa, and the skin on the back of his neck prickled with foreboding.

"Let's go down to the clearing," he said.

Whatever was going to happen, it would be there.

Gracie nodded, her face pale, and the two of them started down the stairs. She paused midway and pointed through the branches, a few creamy rose petals falling upon her sleeve.

"Look." Her voice was hushed. "The barrier has reached the clearing."

It was true. The green glow had come to the very edge of the grass. It encircled the oak, crouching there like a watchful sentinel. And at the base of the tree…

He squinted, then swore softly under his breath. A pyre had been built, a stack of branches that rose a good six feet in the air. Upon that bier, dressed all in white, Nissa lay. Her long hair was unbound and her eyes were closed. The magpie perched by her feet, its head bowed.

Alarm spiked through him. He raced down the stairs two at a time, with Gracie right behind him. They rounded the trunk and halted before the unlit pyre. Hayden reached up to tug on the witch's arm.

"What are you doing?" he asked. "Nissa? Come down."

There was no response. Her arm remained limp, as though she were asleep. Or ensorcelled.

The magpie let out a low, mournful whistle, tilting its head to look at them from one beady eye. Overhead, dark clouds raced across the sky, blotting out the sun. These were no normal clouds, however. Their undersides were tinted a sickly greenish color, and the air held an acrid smell.

"The Stone," Gracie said, looking past him at the oak. "It's waking."

The hairs on the back of his neck prickling, Hayden slowly turned. The curtain of foliage that normally hid the Stone was gone as if it had evaporated, and the rock itself was alive with green fire. Brilliant emerald light raced and whirled in the runes, pulsing so brightly that he had to squint to look at it.

Even as they watched, a thin line of green fire raced from the base of the stone to the pyre. A heartbeat later, the bottom branches caught fire.

"It's going to burn her up," Gracie whispered. "She's the sacrifice. Not us."

Cold understanding swept through him: Nissa's sorrows and silences took on new meaning, and the words she'd spoken when she'd thought he was unconscious were suddenly, starkly clear in his mind.

She was the one the Stone would take, not them. And Gracie was fated to take her place as the Witch of the Woods.

A hole opened in his heart—one side filled with love for his sister, the other with what might have been between him and Nissa. What still might be.

"No," he said roughly. "I won't lose you both."

He pivoted and grabbed Nissa's arm, pulling her unresponsive body off the pyre and into his arms.

The wind rose with a sudden wail and the magpie flew up with a squawk of alarm, black and white wings beating in a flurry. Overhead, the branches creaked ominously, the leaves whipped by the wind. As the green flames rose, burning midway up the pyre, Hayden and Gracie retreated.

"Back to the common room?" his sister asked.

"Too dangerous. Look at that wind." The branches of the

oak were lashing back and forth, the wind tossing the flowerpots to the ground and dashing the hanging baskets aside.

A sudden gust stripped petals and fruit from the planters.

"Oh no—the garden!" Gracie cried.

One box tipped, spilling dirt and potatoes as it fell to shatter on the far side of the oak. The dark clouds circled above them, centered over the tree. The pyre blazed, burning a hot, bright emerald. Overhead, the magpie circled, shrieking its danger call.

"Get back," he said, carrying Nissa away from the oak. "Get behind me."

All around the clearing, the barrier sizzled and hissed. The wind intensified, the air filled with torn foliage and shredded flowers. Debris whirled past—the shredded remains of pots, baskets, and vegetable planters. He bent over, trying to shelter Nissa from the worst of it and block the wind from his sister.

Then the pyre exploded in a blaze of green fire.

A moment later, a wailing cry arose, an eerie keening that scraped the inside of his skull. It was the sound of an angry, ancient hunger that would not be denied.

A shrieking gust clawed through the tree, pulling loose the highest room and tossing it to the ground. The structure landed with a sickening crunch, a sound like breaking bone. They flinched back as pieces of wood scattered, tossed into the air by the storm.

"Look," Gracie said, her voice shaking. "The Stone is trying to find Nissa."

Green fire raced out from the base of the tree, the hungry flames leaving charred grasses in their wake as they quested forward. The wind howled, tearing at his aerie and fanning the blaze. Black smoke billowed into the air, the stench making them cough. It was the smell of decay, of hopelessness. Of everything lost.

The tree was no shelter. And they couldn't pass through the impenetrable wall of magic that ringed the clearing. Wildly, Hayden glanced around, his gaze falling on the last place he ever thought would be a refuge.

"The oven." Holding Nissa close, he ran over to the mounded stones.

Eyes wide with apprehension, Gracie hurried after him.

"We have to get inside," he said. "Now."

His sister wrenched open the rounded wooden door, the heartwood cured by fire to withstand the heat of the oven. Would it be strong enough to hold back the enchanted flames?

He set the witch down just outside the door, then ducked through the opening into the dark enclosure. The sudden quiet inside the oven made him aware of his own harsh breathing,

"Take her feet," he told his sister as he grabbed Nissa under the arms.

The green fire surged forward, spitting sparks.

"Gracie!" he yelled. "Get in!"

She jumped into the oven and together they tugged Nissa inside, folding her knees so she'd fit. In his haste, he stumbled backward, thwacking his head on the low stones. The moment the witch's feet cleared the threshold, Gracie scrambled forward and pulled the oven door shut.

Faint light filtered down from the few airholes beside the chimney. His head pounding Hayden crouched beside Nissa, and Gracie knelt on her other side. There was scarcely enough room for the three of them.

For a moment, everything was still. Then Nissa let out a low moan and opened her eyes. She blinked in confusion, her gaze going from Gracie to Hayen.

"No," she said weakly, struggling to sit. "Let me go. The Stone—"

"Can find its own dinner," he said shortly. "I'm not letting the fire take you."

"You don't understand. The sacrifice must be made." She gestured toward the oven door, now outlined in green light. "This is how it ends. This is how it *always* ends."

Her gaze locked with his, and in her clear, sorrow-filled eyes, he saw something that made his heart ache.

"I won't accept that."

She let out a little sound of grief, then lifted her chin. "You have to. Either the Stone takes me, or it takes us all."

"I won't let it." Gracie grabbed her hand. "Is it a curse? Can we break it?"

"I..." The witch hesitated.

Outside, the wind rose to a roar. The light turned green, washing their skin to the color of death, and suddenly the stones surrounding them were warm. Too warm.

Nissa leaned forward, staring at the door, and Hayden grabbed her shoulders.

"Don't open it," he warned.

She shivered, despite the heat, then slumped back against him. "It's too late. The Stone will devour us all now, if it can. I'm sorry."

"Ow." Gracie crouched, balancing on the balls of her feet. "It's getting hot."

"We have to endure it," he said. "Nissa, can you do anything?"

"I'll try." She set one palm to the floor, then winced and quickly pulled it away from the hot stone.

"Get on my back," he said, drawing her to him. "Gracie, in my arms. I'll hold you both off the floor."

"But what about you?" his sister asked.

"My boots are sturdy. I'll be fine." He didn't mention the heat already seeping uncomfortably through the soles. "Hurry."

He boosted Nissa onto his back. After a brief hesitation, she twined her arms around his neck. Then, still crouching, he hoisted Gracie into his arms.

"Stop wiggling," he told her. "Hold onto my waist."

Sweat began trickling down his temples, his thighs burning with the weight of carrying both women. But he wouldn't let either of them go.

Beyond the oven, a howl arose, louder than hungry wolves, an angry cry that clawed at his ears. Nissa shuddered on his back and almost lost her grip, and his sister flinched.

"Hold tight," he gasped. "Both of you."

"How long?" Gracie whispered.

"I will tell you when it's safe." Nissa's voice caught, as if on a sob. As if she couldn't believe that they might, in fact, emerge alive.

CHAPTER 13

They were trapped in the dark bubble of sweltering heat. Though he was strong, Hayden's legs soon began to shake from the strain of holding Nissa on his back and Gracie in his arms. But he refused to set either of them down. The floor of the oven was unbearably hot. He could tell his feet were blistering within his boots as the heat from the walls pressed in on them.

Stand, he told himself, and gritted his teeth while sweat poured down his face and slicked his sides.

Emerald fire flickered around the door, trying to find its way inside. Whenever a tendril of green won through one of the cracks, he heard Nissa mutter a spell, and it vanished.

At last, the heat was too much. He swayed, his legs beginning to buckle.

"Climb up on me, when I fall," he whispered hoarsely to Gracie.

"Never." She gave him a fierce look. "It's almost over."

Almost wasn't soon enough. With agonizing slowness, he collapsed.

"No!" Nissa cried.

He felt the weight of her leave his shoulders, even as Gracie squirmed out of his grasp. Light assaulted his senses as she kicked the door open. His palms hit the searing floor, but he was too tired to do more than hiss in pain.

"Come *on*," his sister said, yanking at his shoulders. "Move, you big oaf!"

Then Nissa set her hands to his backside and gave him a mighty push. The three of them tumbled out of the oven, onto a carpet of charred black grass.

The eldritch fire was gone.

Numbly, Hayden flopped onto his back and stared at the sky. Clouds still roiled over the clearing, but they were a normal, sullen gray. Even as he watched, the wind pushed them apart, showing glimpses of blue beyond.

"Get his boots off," Nissa said, already untying Hayden's laces. "I can heal the damage, if it's not too late."

Gracie joined her, the two of them working quickly. When they pulled his shoes off, agony shot through him. He caught the scream behind his teeth, refusing let it out, and kept his gaze focused on Nissa's face. He heard his sister whimper at the sight of his ravaged feet, but the witch never flinched.

Holding her palms just above either foot, she began to chant. Cool blue light gathered on her hands, then began to drift down over his soles. Fire turned to ice, the relief from pain almost as shocking as his injury. He pulled in a sharp breath of wonder.

"It's working," Gracie said, staring at the witch's hands.

Silently, Nissa nodded. She remained at his feet a moment more, then began working her way up his body. Wherever her light fell, ease followed. His scalded palms cooled, the fierce burns upon his skin receded.

When her hands skimmed his cheeks, he reached up and caught her fingers. Startled, her gaze met his, her white-gold hair falling in a curtain about her face. The blue light faltered, her intent expression easing as the spell faded. She did not try to move away.

"Why?" she asked, her voice low. "Why did you save me?"

"I couldn't let you burn."

A shadow of wings fell over them, and with a whistle and a chirp, the magpie landed beside Nissa on the charred grass. It was all white, now, except for a few black feathers along its wings.

Blushing, the witch pulled her hands from his and looked at the bird.

"Hello, old friend," she said to it. "I'm glad to see you survived, too."

"Who is it?" Gracie asked, scooting to his side as Hayden levered himself to sitting.

"The former Witch of the Woods," Nissa said.

Frowning, Gracie glanced from her to the magpie. "But we broke the curse. Didn't we?"

"We certainly broke the house," he said, glancing over at the wreckage that used to be the magical, garden-surrounded treehouse. "Is it ruined?"

"The cycle is broken." Nissa stared at the tree, a deep melancholy in her expression. "The Stone's power is gone. I am the last Witch of the Woods."

The magpie hopped forward with a cluck, as if in agreement.

"If the Stone is broken," Gracie asked, "then why is she still a bird?"

"That's my fault." Nissa reached over and gently stroked the magpie's back. "Like you, I could not bear to simply stand by and watch as the Stone took its sacrifice. But unlike you, I could not save my mentor. At the very moment when the fire consumed her and the magic came to me, I cast a spell, binding her spirit to this place. I suppose you could call it a curse, though she has never hated me for it."

The bird hopped up into Nissa's lap and chirped once, its bright eye fixed upon her face. She let out a sigh, then looked back at him.

"You are free now, too," she said softly. "The Stone has crumbled, the barrier is gone. There is no reason for you and Gracie to stay."

"There is every reason," Hayden caught her gaze. "I can't speak for Gracie, though I think she'll agree, but everything I need is right here."

From the corner of his eye, he saw his sister nodding vigorously.

"But the garden is gone," Nissa said, sounding confused. "The rooms are all destroyed."

Gently, he reached and took her hand in his. "You're still here."

Her brows drew together. "What could you possibly want from one ill-tempered witch?"

"I'd like to see what kind of life we might make together."

Their gazes locked, and he saw some of her sorrow and loneliness recede, replaced by a tentative hope.

"Please?" he said softly. "Will you try? We could be a family, the three of us."

After a long moment, she nodded. "I will. You and Gracie have become dear to me."

"Hooray!" Gracie cried, then rose and tried unsuccessfully to brush the soot off her clothing. "I'm glad you've both come to your senses. But we should get to work. There's a lot to do to repair the house and gardens."

At her words, the magpie took to the air, brilliant white against the blackened devastation around them. As it flew, it began to sing – a lilting, liquid sound of hope, and redemption. It circled the clearing, and in its wake the grasses greened and small daisies opened their white petals, as though awaking from a slumber.

Hayden stood and pulled Nissa to her feet, then took his sister's hand. The three of them watched in amazement as the bird flew in wide spirals around the tree. The broken branches mended themselves, the withered leaves returned to a glossy green. Starting at the bottom, the shattered steps mended, vines springing up and winding in a profusion of blossoms and berries around the railing.

The pots and baskets jumped back into place, burgeoning with vegetables, the cracked windows of the common room gleamed anew. Before their eyes, the treetop aeries reformed, their sweeping angles and high roofs reappearing as if they'd never been dashed to the ground by furious magic.

The magpie flew up, and up, still singing. As it passed, every branch and board, every plant and flower was restored. It paused at the very top of the oak for a moment, letting out a final, high trill that shook glittering motes of light over the tree, the house, the clearing, and the upturned faces of the mortals below.

Then, between one blink and the next, it disappeared.

"Goodbye, my friend," Nissa whispered, her eyes bright with tears. "Thank you."

"Is she really gone?" Gracie asked.

"Yes. She is freed at last. And so am I." Nissa turned to Hayden, sorrow and worry echoing in her eyes. "She spent the last of our shared magic to restore our home. I… am no longer the Witch of the Woods."

He smiled down at her. "That doesn't matter. You'll always be the woman I want to spend my life with."

Then he bent and kissed her softly on the lips.

A warm breeze, redolent with roses and raspberries, wound about the clearing. The last spark of magic brushed the cheeks of the three humans standing before their enchanted home, then swirled up to gently shake the leaves of the oak tree in farewell. Then up, higher still, above the dark evergreens of the forest, above the small hut at the far edge where a widower wept for his lost children, above the land where the snow drifted softly and people laughed with relief around their bountiful tables.

It soared higher, above the clouds, to the place where light gives way to dark. Up, and up, until it was only a bright speck in the sky—a new and nameless star, shining its quiet blessing over the shadowed world below.

~ * ~

ACKNOWLEDGMENTS

Special thanks, again, goes out to every single backer of the Faerie Hearts Kickstarter campaign. This book wouldn't have happened without you.

Thanks to Mari C. Bell for the excellent brainstorming on The Witch of the Woods - for working with me on the fairytale inspiration, and for naming the characters and envisioning their physical characteristics. I hope I was able to honor your experience as an architect and permaculture gardener, as well as the pieces of your own story which you shared with me.

Grateful thanks to Mercedes Lackey and John Helfers for allowing me to include *The Gift of Love*, which first appeared in the Valdemar anthology Seasons.

And finally, my warmest thank-you to my husband, Lawson, my own creek-eyed prince and true love, for all these many years of adventures big and small. Your support keeps me going.

ALSO BY ANTHEA SHARP

Discover more enchanting short stories!

~ SHORT STORY COLLECTIONS ~
TALES OF FEYLAND & FAERIE
TALES OF MUSIC & MAGIC
THE FAERIE GIRL & OTHER TALES
THE PERFECT PERFUME & OTHER TALES

The *USA TODAY* bestselling FEYLAND Series
High-tech gaming meets the Realm of Faerie

THE DARK REALM
THE BRIGHT COURT
THE TWILIGHT KINGDOM
SPARK
ROYAL
MARNY

~THE DARKWOOD CHRONICLES~
The hidden world of the Dark Elves is discovered by a mortal girl... romance and adventure ensue~

ELFHAME – Book 1
HAWTHORNE – Book 2
RAINE – Book 3

~ THE DARKWOOD TRILOGY ~

WHITE AS FROST

BLACK AS NIGHT

RED AS FLAME

~ VICTORIA ETERNAL ~

Victorian Steampunk meets Space Opera!

STAR COMPASS

STARS & STEAM

COMETS & CORSETS

ABOUT THE AUTHOR

Growing up on fairy tales and computer games, *USA Today* bestselling author Anthea Sharp enjoyed melding the two in her award-winning, bestselling Feyland series, which has sold over 150k copies worldwide.

In addition to the fae fantasy/cyberpunk mashup of Feyland, she also writes Victorian Spacepunk, and fantasy romance. Her books have won awards and topped bestseller lists, and garnered over 1.2 million reads at Wattpad. Her short fiction has appeared in Fiction River, DAW anthologies, The Future Chronicles, and Beyond The Stars: At Galaxy's edge, as well as many other publications.

Anthea splits her time between sunny climes and the story-inspiring forests of the Pacific Northwest. Contact her at antheasharp@hotmail.com or visit her website – www.antheasharp.com

Anthea also writes historical romance under the pen name Anthea Lawson. Find out about her acclaimed Victorian romantic adventure novels at www.anthealawson.com.

Be the first to hear about new releases and reader perks by subscribing to Anthea's newsletter, Sharp Tales.

Made in the USA
Monee, IL
14 January 2025